TO KILL A FAE

HOLLOWCLIFF DETECTIVES BOOK 1

C.S. WILDE

CHAPTER 1

IN MERA'S EXPERIENCE, three things motivated a murder: secrets, convenience, or passion. Yet, as she observed the dead fae king sprawled on the living room floor, eyes and mouth agape as if he were about to scream for his life—no pun intended—she couldn't help but wonder if there might be a fourth.

She didn't know which of the fae kings this one might be. Many lived in fancy penthouses or villas in the fae borough, Tir Na Nog, each with their own nasty courts. And yet, this particular king had died in human territory, which made the case puzzling to say the least.

Fae didn't get along with… well, basically the entire country, but at least they showed some degree of respect for witches, vamps, and shifters. Humans, though? Nothing more than weak, pitiful beings. The regent of the fae state had said it point blank during a speech on live TV a year ago. Sure, the assface had been impeached from the council immediately after that, but the faeries' cold indifference remained.

It was ironic that this dead king had died with a human woman by his side.

Oh, the horror. The shame.

No wonder the Cap had rushed all detectives available to the scene.

Hollowcliff was the Capital of Tagrad, and it was split into five non-bordering boroughs, each the capital of their respective state—witches, vamps, shifters, humans, and fae. But Tir Na Nog made the rest of Hollowcliff their bitches, which didn't seem fair, considering they were corrupt as fuck and didn't exactly abide by Tagradian law. Still, the spoiled assholes were rarely punished because they had so much power.

This meant that Mera and her peers had to gather as much evidence as possible on the murder scene before those fae dickwarts claimed it. Never mind that a human had died here today. Once the *pixies* took over, no one would care about bringing her murderer to justice.

So yeah, Mera and her partner, Julian—plus the four detectives currently on scene—had to hurry.

Stepping beside her, Julian ran a hand over his smooth hair, which had the color of ripe lemons. "What do you think, Mer? Lovers' quarrel?"

Her throat suddenly dried at the sight of him.

Julian might be human, but he looked nearly ethereal. Like those marbled statues of the old gods, he was made of perfectly straight lines and sharp cuts. His strong, defined muscles were easy to spot, even covered by a white T-shirt and brown leather jacket.

Forced to clear her throat, she focused on the bodies—the king lying belly up and the woman resting on her stomach, reaching for him.

Almost poetic.

Too poetic.

"It seems that way," she muttered.

The victim wore a fancy silken shirt and golden pants. With his trimmed beard and pointy ears crowded with golden hooped earrings—talk about bad taste in fashion—he resembled a pirate with a glitter obsession. Certainly not a king.

Maybe he belonged to the Unseelie Courts. Then again, few people outside of Tir Na Nog knew what the Unseelie looked like, and Mera wasn't one of them.

A whistle escaped Julian's puckered lips. "A fae and a human. That's kind of forbidden. Unofficially, that is." His curious gaze traveled around the apartment. "Weird. Those snobby assholes should be here by now."

Even though Tagrad was governed by a council of one representative from each state, all five with equal weight in decision making—*yeah, sure*—it was clear who the richest and strongest player was: the jackasses from Tir Na Nog.

Julian was right. It was odd that they weren't here.

Pulling out a small notepad from the pocket in his vest, he began to read it. "Rigor mortis sets the time of death to six hours ago for him, and ten for her. A neighbor heard a man scream last night, but didn't think much of it."

The woman had been dead already, which meant she hadn't reached out to the king as she died. She'd been positioned that way.

"The female is Sara Hyland, twenty-two." Julian nodded toward the woman's body. "Attended UCH, but lived here on the weekends, and during school break. The apartment belongs to the parents. She had a history of bringing in stray... *gentlemen*."

"Maybe one of them got jealous," Mera guessed, but deep down she knew the chances were slim. More of a gut feeling than fact, yet over the years, she'd learned to trust her instincts.

3

"The door was half open when the neighbor came down this morning to check on her," Julian added. "She found them this way."

"Convenient."

He arched one thick, brown eyebrow at her. "You think the neighbor did it?"

Mera had seen the neighbor, a ninety-year-old human without a bone of magic in her body. Not a shifter, not a bloodsucker or a witch, and definitely not a fae. Those Mera could tell from a distance, even when they disguised themselves.

Glancing at Julian, she admired the freckles that spread atop the bridge of his nose. "No, she definitely didn't do it."

Mera forced herself to look away from him, because the man was like the sun: beautiful, majestic, and if one stared for too long, they might go blind. She'd been working at the precinct for three years, but she'd never told Julian about her feelings for him.

It sucked, because he was not only her partner but also her best friend.

She wanted to kiss him senseless and do things with him, things she normally did with her profusion of one-night stands—the only type of relationship Mera could afford.

The Cap's voice rang in her mind. *"Hide who you are, and you might survive, cookie."*

Mera could never be with Julian. He deserved better than what she could give.

'We should have sex with him,' the lustful, ravenous force inside her whispered. *'Just to check if he lives up to the expectations.'*

And then what? Her rational self argued.

'Just once.' The siren side of her grinned, the cheeky feeling spreading through Mera's chest. After all, her siren

essence was always there, with her, even when her magic was dormant. That horny bastard...

Down, girl, Mera thought, fighting her siren urges.

"You won't believe her cause of death, though," Julian offered, snatching her attention.

The fae king's demise was obvious—a silver stake to the heart. A death fueled by hate and convenience. Which raised the question, why did Sara Hyland have such a fine weapon in her apartment?

Sara's death, on the other hand, wasn't so simple.

Mera should feign ignorance. She had to hide anything that might give away her secret, otherwise, she would be hunted to death by every creature in Tagrad. After all, having a common enemy had been the sole reason for the unification.

And that's what Mera was. Their enemy.

"The woman drowned," she blurted, because she really, *really* craved Julian's attention.

Crap.

Mera had seen enough humans drowning to know what a body looked like after the deed. The woman's closed eyes were slightly swollen, so were her lips. The tip of her purplish tongue peeked out of her mouth, and thin veins peppered her milky white skin, which meant she hadn't stayed underwater for long after her death, just long enough.

A small grin hooked up Julian's left cheek as he blinked at her. "Damn, partner. Right as always. I honestly couldn't believe when forensics said it. She doesn't look like she drowned."

She did, actually.

"It's strange, isn't it?" he asked, facing the bodies. "Why would someone bother to drown her, dry her up, and lay her here?"

"Bait," Mera said simply, more out of instinct than anything else.

"Think like a predator," her mother's bitter voice echoed in her ears. *"Become the predator."*

Well, fuck that bitch and the six feet above her.

"You can't come in here!" Officer Pearlmann yelled from the corridor, near the apartment's entrance.

"I can do whatever I want," a strong, and somewhat regal voice countered.

By the way the thin hairs on Mera's arm stood, whoever he was, he had magic in him. A crapload of it.

Fae. Definitely fae.

Sirens, much like sharks, had an acute sense of smell, and everyone's magic smelled differently.

His power flowed from him with steady might, but it smelled crisp and fresh, like a dewy night or a foggy morning. A gentle scent for a ruthless power.

'He has the kind of voice you want to fuck,' the siren inside her remarked.

Mera rolled her eyes and sighed.

Slut.

'Why, thank you.'

The sound of a hard shove reached her, and then steps thumped closer on the wooden floor, but suddenly stopped.

"You can't take this case from us." Pearlman must have stood in the fae's way. "A human was murdered in here."

More pushing and shoving echoed, followed by someone hitting the floor with a harsh thud. Poor Pearlman, but considering what a fae could do, he'd been lucky.

Mera exchanged one glance with Julian as she felt—and heard—the fae stomping from behind. Her partner winked at her but remained quiet; a silent message that said, *"We got this."*

"Danu in the fucking prairies," the fae grumbled as he

stepped between them. "Are all humans as stupid as your colleague?"

"I don't know. Are all *pixies* assholes like you?" She turned to him and regretted it immediately.

The fae was at least two heads taller than her, and even Julian, who was tall for a human, stood a head shorter than him.

It wasn't just his height, though. Fae were generally beautiful, but this male was simply otherworldly. Pointy ears poked out of a mane of moonlight-silver hair, which was tied back in a loose and messy bun atop his head, allowing thin strings to frame his face. His deep caramel skin contrasted immensely with blue eyes that were clearer than the sky.

His body was different from Julian's. Strong yet lean. His muscles weren't as evident as her partner's, but still intimidating. She could see it by the rolled-up sleeves that showcased corded, and way-too-appealing forearms. Like he was a panther about to prowl. She could picture the rest of him from underneath the white shirt, gray checkered vest, and suit pants he wore—well, her siren did, that lustful jackass.

Mera's breathing became shallow. The siren cheered.

The fae's brow creased with a frown as he studied Mera from head to toe, something shining in those feral blue eyes. His focus roamed over her russet hair, going past her green irises, down to her shirt and leather jacket, navy jeans, until it finally settled on her boots.

He couldn't discover the truth simply by looking at her… could he?

A cold sweat broke on her skin, but she had to get her shit together. No magical creature had ever been able to tell that Mera was a siren, including a handful of fae.

He grinned, seeming satisfied with his appraisal of her. "Mera Maurea?"

She nodded, mostly because words failed her—either

from his magnetic presence, or the sheer horror of what he might've found within her.

Without another word, he turned back to Julian. "Julian Smith, I assume?"

Her partner saluted him with a middle finger. "Yeah. And you are?"

"Sebastian Dhay." Ignoring Julian's offense, he shoved both hands in the pockets of his tailored pants. "But you can call me Bast."

With his suit and impeccable brown leather shoes, he only needed a golden pocket watch to complete the old-school, rich-boy vibe. Remarkable, really, that this was the standard uniform for Tir Na Nog detectives.

He resembled either a dandy or a douche. Definitely a douche.

"I'm here to investigate the murder of Zev Ferris, king of the Summer Court," Bast informed them.

Mera's jaw dropped. "You're telling me that this guy," she pointed at the victim, "who is dressed like a leprechaun merchant, is a light court king? Are you serious?"

Bast gave her a dashing grin, his teeth whiter than his hair. "Not everyone can dress well, sugar tits." He ogled her jeans, white shirt, and leather jacket as if trying to prove his point.

She glared at him as a furious blush rose to her cheeks. "Sorry if I don't dress to your dandy standards, *pixie*."

Mera felt the siren's eyes rolling, even if she was the siren and the siren was her. *'Wow. Good one. He called us sugar tits, and that's what we hit him with? Pixie?'*

The bastard had a point.

A loud laugh burst from Bast's lips before he turned to Julian. "Your partner is most intriguing, isn't she?"

Julian's arms remained crossed, not an inch of amusement on his face. "You disrespect the lady again, and you and I will have a problem, asshole."

Bast's grin was wild and savage. The image of a panther came to mind again. "*You* will have a problem, human. I'll simply call it entertainment."

On the upside, though, Bast's condescending attitude meant he must think she was human. Mera let out a relieved breath, then surveyed the room, noticing the lack of a team of fae invading their crime scene.

"The king of the Summer Court is dead, and you're here alone?" she asked. "Where's the cavalry?"

Bast shook his index finger at her. "Not bad, sugar tits."

Before she could scream at him, he raised his hands in surrender. "I meant no disrespect." He pointed at her breasts. "They're nice, perky, and about the right size. It's a compliment," he assured, giving her a thumbs up.

A fucking thumbs up.

She would kill this bastard today.

"Call me sugar tits again, and I swear I will bite off your fingers one by one, dickwart."

'Ah, much better!' Her siren clapped.

His silver eyebrows arched, and his eyes glinted with mischief. For a fleeting moment, Mera saw something inside him, something ancient and dark, but then it was gone. "Is that a promise, *kitten?*"

What an unnerving fartface! But at least he'd stopped calling her sugar tits.

"I'll be honest with you two," Bast went on, barely addressing Julian, his focus solely on Mera. "We want discretion on this one. Your captain traded that for minimum interference from our side. So, here I am."

Oh, the Cap. Ruth. The fiercest woman Mera knew. That she'd managed to strike a deal with the fae district was nothing short of a miracle. Humans had few bargaining chips when it came to those fuckers, but Ruth had plenty of tricks up her sleeve.

"Great," Mera conceded. "Try not to stand in our way, and—"

"You don't understand. I'm not here to assist you both. I'm here," he pointed at Mera, "because I'm your new partner."

CHAPTER 2

MERA BARGED into the Cap's office and nearly blasted the door closed behind her.

"I did *not* agree to this!"

Ruth didn't raise her attention from the papers she was signing. Sitting behind her carved mahogany desk with her white uniform, and blond-going-silver hair in a cropped cut, she looked nothing short of a general. Or a mountain of ice.

Hard to tell.

Mera's chest heaved while she stood in the middle of the room, air puffing through her nostrils as she waited for a reaction.

"Are you under the impression that you have a say in it?" the Cap asked, her tone dangerously flat, like that time Mera escaped to a party when she was fifteen. Once she returned, Ruth asked if she'd had any fun before grounding her for a whole month. But Mera wasn't a kid anymore, and she wouldn't budge.

"Julian is my partner, not that damn pixie."

"That's a derogatory term."

"They call us worse." Mera slammed both hands on her

waist and spun around. "Cap, the murder happened in our jurisdiction, and—"

"First of all, *you* are not *us*, and second, you're smart enough to understand how things work in Tagrad."

True.

Slowly laying down her pen, the Cap intertwined her hands atop her desk. "Mera, you're the best detective I have. Julian comes second. Also, I believe I taught you the meaning of compromise?"

"Yes, ma'am," she answered quietly.

"Then you know that you're in your current situation because I had to…?"

Mera crossed her arms, studying her own boots. "Compromise."

"Good." Her attention returned to her papers. "Now, if there's nothing else—"

"Ruth." Mera's tone lowered to a whisper. "He might find out."

The woman watched her from below nearly white eyebrows. "No fae ever has. I worked your ID, and hired the warlock to hide your siren magic. I took you as my own, cookie. I wouldn't put you in danger. Trust me, you'll be fine."

The memory of the one time Mera asked the Cap, *"What if the warlock blabs?"* returned.

Ruth had watched her without a hint of emotion, not giving a single clue as to what she might be thinking.

"He won't," she finally assured.

"How can you be so certain?" Mera insisted.

"You don't need to know."

The Cap would never kill someone to protect her, of that Mera was certain. Ruth had the biggest sense of duty, and the highest morals in the entire force, but there were other ways of making sure secrets were kept hidden. If anything, the Cap was resourceful.

Kind, too.

She had adopted Mera when everyone else would have either killed her on the spot or called the cops. She owed the woman *everything*.

"I wouldn't send you on this mission if I thought you might be exposed," Ruth continued. "Your partner for this assignment will be Detective Dhay. And I expect your full cooperation."

"But⬝"

"I think working this case with a fae will do us some good," the Cap went on, always bordering that line between sweet mother and fierce boss. "Maybe it'll improve relations between the two boroughs. Who knows?"

Ha, dream on.

When the Cap raised an eyebrow at her, Mera wondered if she'd said it out loud. Sometimes she swore Ruth could read her thoughts.

"Go solve this case, Detective." Once more, she focused on the papers. "That's an order."

Mera didn't trust easily, but she trusted the Cap with her life. Literally. She also knew better than to poke a sleeping tiger with a short stick.

When Mera stepped out of the office, Bast was waiting for her with a smug look on his stupidly beautiful face. He leaned over a table, arms crossed, and chin held high as if he'd won a battle.

Julian stood beside him, his hazel eyes asking and a little desperate.

Walking toward her partner, Mera bit her bottom lip. "You'll have to sit this one out, Jules." Her hand rested on his shoulder and he immediately cupped it with his own.

Electricity crackled down Mera's spine and pooled at her

belly, but she was used to this. It was how she felt every time Julian touched her.

"Will you be careful?" he asked, his fingers intertwining with hers.

She winked at him. "When am I not careful?"

"Only always."

"Are you two lovebirds done?" Bast nodded to the exit of the precinct. "Detective Maurea and I have work to do."

"Mind your own business, *pixie*," Julian spat, the bitterness in his tone so intense that it pricked Mera's tongue.

Bast frowned, but that typical fae wickedness came to the surface again, flickering behind his eyes. A hint of a smile brushed his lips. "Are you jealous? Rest assured, I'll take good care of your partner."

"Buddy, Mer would never go for one of you," Julian countered without hesitating. "She prefers her males real and without magic."

Not true. Mera had slept with a warlock yesterday, and a wolf shifter not a week ago, but Jules had no clue. It was not like she told him about her romantic conquests—if fleeting one-night stands fit the definition.

"Glad I struck a nerve, *Jules.*" Bast turned to Mera with an air of madness, but he must've spotted the concern on her face, because he cleared his throat, and whatever had been there a moment ago vanished. He pulled down the edges of his vest and fixed his collar. "Shall we, *kitten?*"

"Call me that again, and I'll shove my gun up your ass, dickface."

"Such unneeded brutality. Try and see things from my perspective, *kitten.* I don't have many options left." He gave Julian a wink. "*Mer* is already taken."

Julian flipped him the bird, but Bast didn't seem to mind.

"Fucking fae," Mera grumbled to herself as she pulled

Bast away, toward the exit of the precinct. Raising a hand, she waved. "Talk to you later, Jules."

As soon as they stepped out on the street, she let Bast go and pointed one finger at him. "Here's how we'll do this. You won't try to fool me, you'll share information, and you'll play nice. Understood?"

"Loud and clear, except for the part about playing nice." He spread a hand over his chest in an apologetic manner. "Not in my nature, you see."

She rolled her eyes. "Whatever. So, I usually go to the family first—"

"What? That's moronic." A strand of silver hair slipped over the left side of Bast's face, and he tucked it behind his pointy ear. "Did you tell your parents anything when you were Sara Hyland's age?"

Mera's situation growing up had been… *different*.

She didn't have a father because her mother said Mera had been born of Poseidon, which was utter bullshit since gods weren't real—fae, human, Atlantean, or whatever. Also, confiding in the woman who beat her senseless on a weekly basis didn't make much sense.

She did confide in the Cap, though.

Ruth had found Mera when she was only thirteen. She'd saved her in every sense of the word, so Mera never hid anything from her, simply because she didn't have to. She'd even told Ruth about that time she'd let Billy Wetzel grope her in the parking lot, which hadn't been one of Mera's proudest moments.

"The woman who raised me kept an open line of communication. So yes, I told her everything. How about you?"

He stared at her as if she'd come from another planet. "I'm fae. We don't trust easily." He studied his fancy shoes, and his voice grew quieter. "Especially our own."

She could certainly relate.

Bast did have a point, though. If they were going to solve this case quickly, so that Mera could be back on the streets with Julian, she would have to throw standard procedure out the window.

"Fine," she gave in begrudgingly. "On to the friends list it is."

Mera stopped before the limestone construction that resembled an old castle. It had rococo carvings of humans, witches, fae, shifters, and vamps lining the windowsills and door. The steep, red-tiled roof was carefully crafted, and matched perfectly with the medieval vibe of the four-story building.

Artsy vamps from Kazania loved detailed and excessive crap like this, so she wouldn't be surprised if one of them had been the architect. These types of constructions were a rarity in Clifftown, where most buildings were block houses or skyscrapers. Yes, the human borough had earned the title *concrete jungle*, and although most humans took that with pride, Mera guessed the other boroughs hadn't meant it as a compliment.

"UCH—University College of Hollowcliff" hung in big brown letters atop the university's stone façade, arching over the large wooden entrance.

Every borough had a branch of UCH, even Tir Na Nog, but the bigger courts never attended it. Only lower Sidhe and weaker faeries such as brownies, leprechauns, or banshees went to public schools.

Not that Mera had seen it firsthand. She'd never been to the fae state, only heard the Cap's stories from the time she had to escort the human minister on an assignment.

"Sara Hyland studied economics here," Mera said as she watched students strolling across the endless green fields that stretched around the property. "Divide and conquer, *partner?*"

"You tell me," he replied without turning away from the façade. "If you were a civilian, would you open up to a faerie without a human present?"

She observed the stares Bast received from passersby. Some were loaded with hate, others with lust; some were quizzical, and others filled with cold indifference. For the first time, Mera realized how hard being here must be for him. Not that he seemed to mind.

"The issues between our kinds go both ways." He raised his shoulders. "Without a common enemy, the comradery forged in the Great War crumbles with each passing day."

Common enemy.

He meant sirens. Like her.

"You guys don't make liking you any easier," she muttered under her breath.

A laugh twittered in his throat. "That we don't."

Mera couldn't work this case the way she did with a human partner. Which meant that casting a wide net was a no-go. Also, they couldn't waste time on cold leads.

"Roommate?" she asked, removing a pad from the inside pocket of her leather jacket. "Andrea Johnson, room forty-five."

Bast grinned and stepped aside, showing her the way. "After you."

Inside the building they went, passing through crowded halls and corridors, then following the garden path that led to the student quarters. The concrete block stood near the left end of the campus, hidden behind a small forest.

All the while, a metallic scent invaded her nostrils.

Magic.

It was weaker than Bast's and it flickered in and out of range. Mera searched her surroundings, but other than

17

passing students and teachers, she couldn't find anyone suspicious.

"Everything all right?" he asked from beside her.

"Do you feel a magical presence?"

He stopped, closed his eyes and raised his head to the sky, as if he was trying to catch a scent.

Mera noticed how squared his chin was, and the sharp curve his jaw made toward his Adam's apple. And his hair, Poseidon in the trenches, it resembled silver silk. Under the sun, it seemed like thousands of spiders had woven its threads.

"No." He opened his eyes. "I got nothing. Why?"

"I don't know." Shrugging, she let it go. "Gut feeling, I guess."

"You mean insanity," he scoffed. "A human, thinking they can sense magic? That's hilarious."

Mera almost told him to shove it, but she walked a thin line already. Better to let the subject fade.

Once they reached a set of stairs, they went up to the third floor, soon arriving before a door with the number forty-five engraved on it.

After Bast knocked, a short girl with glasses answered. Her eyes were red from crying too much. Her rock band T-shirt smelled of sweat, tears, and Cheetos.

Mera and Bast exchanged a glance.

Bingo.

"Andrea Johnson?" He leaned on the door frame, oozing charm—which wasn't hard for someone as freakishly handsome as him. "We're the detectives in charge of your roommate's murder. We were wondering if you could answer some questions."

"You're a fae," the girl sniffed, her eyes trapped on Bast's face. "Why are you investigating a human murder?"

"Sara Hyland was involved with some of my people. I'm

working with Clifftown's police on this case, as you can see by my human partner."

His tongue was fast and sharp, not that it surprised Mera. Bast's kind was famous for trickery and quick thinking.

He nodded to Andrea's room. "If we may?"

"I-I'm not sure," she stuttered.

"Please?" He smiled and it was over. Mera could practically see the girl's knees melting.

Andrea nodded hastily and stepped aside, letting them into the room.

"Ms. Johnson…" Mera started, observing the space. Two beds rested against each wall, one carefully made, the other a twirling mess of Cheetos bags atop a dirty blanket. At some point, Sara Hyland made her bed and left this room for the weekend, never to return. "Do you know anyone who might want to harm your roommate?"

"Friend," Andrea mumbled. "Sara was my friend. And no, everyone liked her."

A lie. Mera could taste it.

She glanced back to Bast, who'd gone to inspect some papers on a desk near the window. The nod he gave her said he'd also caught the lie, but his focus quickly returned to the documents on the desk.

"Ms. Johnson, you're safe," Mera assured, her tone soft, calming. "Are you certain Sara didn't have any enemies?"

"Yes."

"Was she involved in any illegal activities?"

"Definitely not." She cleared her throat. "Sara was as clean as a whistle."

Ah, there was the lie.

Andrea clearly wanted to protect her friend's memory, but the faster Mera could figure out this case, the faster she'd be back with Julian.

Briefly peeking at Bast, she found him focused on a notebook. This was her chance.

Mera's siren swam underneath her skin, twirling around her vocal cords as she turned to Andrea.

A siren's glamour was more refined than normal glamour, at least that's what the Cap said. Also, the warlock's hiding spell helped. Even if Bast paid attention, he couldn't catch her weakened siren essence. Mera had once interrogated an undocumented banshee, and the poor thing hadn't had a clue.

Why should he be any different?

'He's a Sidhe,' her siren reminded her. *'Crapload more powerful than a banshee.'*

Well, she had to risk it.

Mera's siren spell wove into her voice. "Ms. Johnson, are you sure?"

"I'm…" The girl's eyes widened, and her jaw dropped. "No, I'm lying." She frowned, as if she couldn't understand what came out of her mouth. "Sara had to pay for college. You can't blame her."

"How did she pay her tuition?" Mera pushed.

Andrea shook her head, as if forcing herself awake. "I-I don't know. She had a business."

Mera's siren was about to charge again when Bast stepped beside her, looking at her with puzzled sky-blue eyes.

Her heart stopped. Heck, her lungs froze, too.

Had he sensed her siren essence? Was Mera's life in Hollowcliff over?

Bast watched her a moment longer, then turned to Andrea. "You humans are addicted to your precious technology. Did Sara have a mobile phone?"

Mera felt like she could breathe again, and only then did she notice Bast was holding a black notebook.

"No way," Andrea argued. "Sara was super old school."

Odd. Every human had a phone, including Mera. Yet, Andrea seemed to be telling the truth, at least about this.

"Smart decision, considering your friend's line of work." He wiggled the notebook in front of her. "Your roommate had some important clients, Ms. Johnson. I'm guessing she was dealing drugs?"

"Okay, fine!" Andrea blurted, like she'd been holding a breath for too long.

Apparently, a charming fae was more convincing than Mera's siren, which kind of offended her.

"Wolfsbane, fae crystal," Andrea continued. "She even sold tampered blood to the vamps."

"I see." Bast's slender finger touched the surface of the notebook. "Detective Maurea, this is a list of Sara Hyland's clients." He opened the pad and pointed to a page. "Our fae king is here, plus some big shot vampires and shifters. In theory, any of them could have wanted her dead."

"Detective Dhay!" Mera snapped. "We can't disclose information in front of a civilian."

"Wait. A fae king killed Sara?" the girl asked.

Too late.

Rolling his eyes, Bast snapped his fingers in front of Andrea. She immediately straightened her spine, her eyes wide open. Mera waved in front of her but the girl didn't blink.

"You'll forget what I said about the fae king," he ordered. Maybe Mera had lost her mind, but she could swear his irises had turned black for a quick second. "Understood?"

Andrea nodded robotically, but when he snapped his fingers again, the girl's shoulders relaxed.

She blinked at them, then nodded at the notebook. "That was Sara's."

21

"Now it's ours." He smacked the notebook shut and walked out of the room.

Mera barely had time to give Andrea her card before rushing to catch up with him. "What are you doing?" she asked as she reached him by the stairs. "You can't use magic on a human in Clifftown, not without their approval." She lowered her tone. "It's against the freaking law."

Not that she'd done any better with her glamour, but Bast believed Mera was human, and after over a decade pretending, she'd learned to act the part.

Mostly.

He winked at her as they went down the stairs. "I won't tell if you won't."

She blew an exasperated breath. "At least it's clear why Sara had the silver stake."

"Being cautious is a good trait for a drug dealer, especially when doing business with criminal vampires."

"Do you think a bloodsucker did this?"

"Unlikely. A vampire wouldn't have drowned her." Stopping, he watched Mera. "You know who would, though?"

She shook her head.

"Sirens."

Mera swallowed dry, trying to hide the panic in her tone. "That's impossible."

"Perhaps. But mermaids used to walk among us, way before you and I dreamed of existing. A time before most living creatures in this country." He didn't take his eyes off her as he spoke. "Sure, nowadays they're either exterminated or banished, but there are plenty of them out there, in the sea."

"Yeah, I know," she answered quietly. "They used to have their own borough back in the early days." An ache Mera couldn't explain pricked her chest; a longing for something she'd never had. "Look, sirens are cursed. They can't set foot on Tagrad. Even if Sara was an exceptional swimmer and passed through the protection zone, and even if a siren drowned her, they couldn't have placed her body back in her apartment without crumbling to ashes first."

He narrowed his eyes at Mera for an uncomfortable amount of time. "You're right," he finally spoke, then showed her the notebook and a name. "What do you make of this, then?"

Mera's blood froze. A small earthquake quivered underneath her skin.

The word had been scribbled in messy handwriting below Zev Ferris, and it was half-blotched by what seemed to be a dried tear.

Poseidon.

CHAPTER 3

I<small>T WAS</small> night by the time they returned to Mera's precinct.

Her desk lamp highlighted the word scribbled on the notebook, the name echoing in her mind.

Poseidon. Poseidon. Poseidon.

Okay, whoever was behind the alias couldn't be the actual Poseidon. Like every other deity, he wasn't real.

So, who was the dickface passing for him?

Not a siren, obviously. Mera was the only one in Tagrad —or at least, she had been until now.

If Sara Hyland was smuggling some sort of drug to the merfolk, she would have to sail beyond the protection zone, far into Open Ocean. Which basically meant a death sentence, unless she used one of the bulky government charters that could obliterate an entire school of sirens in the blink of an eye—a death machine birthed by technology *and* magic.

A shiver coursed down Mera's spine as she remembered watching the Nightbringer's hull cut across the surface above her.

She'd hid inside a forest of algae with her best friend, Belinda

Tiderider, and watched the metallic beast's belly break moonlight. It cast a shadow upon her home.

The ocean had never been so silent...

She shook off the memory.

Mera doubted Sara had used a Nightbringer to smuggle drugs. Which begged the question, could there be another siren in Tagrad?

Impossible.

Mera had been the only one to break into the protection zone and survive to tell the tale. If someone before her had done it, Professor Currenter would have known. Everyone would.

Her attention returned to the open case file sprawled on her desk, and she spotted the picture of Sara Hyland's body.

According to the notebook, she was selling tampered blood to Norman Beetes, a big player in Kazania, the vamps' borough. Sara was smart, and kept some leverage within her notes—a must when in bed with terrible people.

Her customers also included Lara Ackerton, a pack queen, and one of the most notorious criminals in Lycannie; Agnes Bessie, a bloodthirsty witch from Evanora; Richard Hegway, the cruelest loan shark in Clifftown, and many others. Sara's notebook probably had enough material to incriminate a third of the low lives in Hollowcliff.

Jules had quickly sent the info to the other boroughs, and taken the lead on Richard's case, the only one in Clifftown's jurisdiction.

Rubbing her forehead, Mera sighed. Why would any of these assholes drown their drug dealer?

"Frustrated much?" Bast asked from behind, reading a newspaper with his feet propped atop Phil's desk. The lamp on the left end of the table shed light into the pages.

He was lucky Phil had already gone home, or he'd be hearing a long speech about "how important it was to respect other officers, and also, get your fucking feet off my desk."

"It would be nice if you were helping me," Mera pointed out, "*partner*."

"I am." He showed her the newspaper's first page, which had a picture of the dead fae king but no mention of Sara Hyland. "I suppose my people struck a deal with your newspapers."

"Oh, the scandal," she mocked. "Not only did the Summer King die in Clifftown, but he died beside a human woman. One must fix what one can."

"And one did," he turned his attention back to the pages. "The death of a fae in human territory is not to be taken lightly, kitten. The relations between the two boroughs have been delicate for decades."

An uneasy feeling settled in her stomach. "Do you think this could be the tipping point?"

"We've gone to war for less," he answered casually. "Shifters and vampires would support you, so would the witches. We have most of the magic, though. And faeries enjoy playing dangerous games." He seemed to consider it. "Hard to predict the outcome."

A new idea suddenly hit her like a hammer. "Maybe the murderer wanted to cause a national incident."

"That's what I thought at first." He frowned at the pages. "But it doesn't add up. Why drown her? Why kill Zev Ferris and place her body next to his, knowing my people would strike a deal with yours to cover up their connection?"

Her hair swayed as she cocked her head left, observing him. "True. Fae can be predictable in their duplicity. In their trickery, too."

He chuckled. "My kind especially."

"Night fae, right?"

He gave her a sideways grin. "What gave it away?"

The darkness in his eyes.

"Your hair. Night fae have hair the color of the moon."

He gave her a humorless smirk. "Someone's been paying attention."

According to the stories the Cap told her, thousands of years ago—before Hollowcliff and the nation of Tagrad existed—the Night and Winter Courts lost a mighty battle against the light fae—Summer, Autumn, and Spring—while the mysterious Day Court chose to remain impartial.

This explained why the Night and Winter Courts held almost no power in the fae state. Why most of Winter lived up north, while Night lived isolated in an island off the coast.

It was also why the winning courts of light occupied the majority of fae territory.

Night fae especially—or nightlings—were despised by their counterparts in Tir Na Nog, yet no one knew what had caused that civil war.

There were rumors, though.

"Is it true you can dab into dark magic?" she probed.

Bast changed the newspaper's page slowly. "I'm a nightling, so yes. Though my magic and the kind you're referring to are not the same. By dark magic, you mean forbidden magic. No one with a shred of common sense dabbles into that. Our magic is dark, as much as Summer and Day's is light." He glanced at her with annoyance. "It's just a term."

"Is it?" She observed his impeccable shirt, vest, and pants. "Why did you become a detective?"

"Am I under interrogation?" he asked carefully, a snarl in his tone.

Message received, but Mera couldn't help herself. "Okay, fine, but don't you find it ironic that you're a night fae and your last name is Dhay?"

"Yes," he retorted without any amusement. "It's fucking hilarious."

She rolled her eyes, then focused on the notebook. "The killer must have known Sara Hyland's murder would lose importance compared to the Summer King's. Maybe they were counting on it."

"If that's the case, why would they bother drowning her?"

He had a point.

The door to the Cap's office opened and Ruth called in Mera. Bast dropped the newspaper atop Phil's desk and followed her, even though he hadn't been invited.

Julian stood inside the office, a concerned look creasing his forehead.

Mera glanced at him and then the Cap. "We got the toxicology reports from the coroner, didn't we?"

"We did," Ruth said as she dropped on her leather chair. "There were no defensive wounds in Sara's body. No paralyzing agents in her blood either, so it's fair to assume she was stupefied by magic while still breathing."

Anger gnawed at Mera's gut. Rendering someone immobile only to drown them with minimal effort was a cowardly way to kill.

The sheer agony Sara must have felt…

"There's more," Julian added, his tone heavy. "She was pregnant. And the fetus had magical DNA, though it's hard to pinpoint what kind of supernatural fathered it."

Something in Mera's chest dropped. This murder got more gruesome by the second. "Okay," she breathed. "So, it's safe to assume the child was Zev Ferris'."

"We're waiting for further DNA results, but yes." The Cap turned to the small squared window on her left, which led to a view of the old, abandoned building across the street.

She always did that when she needed to think.

Stepping forward, Bast stood beside Mera. "The

28

murderer could perform strong magic. That rules out shifters, at least. Vampires can glamour, so they could've stupefied her, but my bet would be on a fae or a witch."

"Great." Mera chortled. "That gives us a pool of what, eighteen million creatures?"

"I wouldn't rule out mermaids," he added.

Bast couldn't drop the damn bone, could he? She had never wanted to smack someone in the face so hard.

"Sirens worship Poseidon," he went on. "It's logical that whoever named themselves Poseidon is a mermaid. Also, a siren could've paralyzed Sara by speaking, or using the macabre."

"Detective Dhay." The Cap narrowed her eyes at him, a freezing storm in her tone. "If mermaids step foot in Hollow-cliff—no, in all of Tagrad, they disintegrate. Literally. So no, mermaids are not a viable angle."

Oh, how Mera loved this woman.

"With all due respect, Captain,—"

"There's more," Julian interrupted, running a hand through his lemon-colored hair. "The contents of Sara Hyland's lungs, more specifically, the composition of the water in which she drowned, doesn't match with Clifftown's shore."

The Cap leaned forward and rested her elbows on the table, forming a triangle with her hands. "They match the lower end of the eastern shore."

Fae state.

More precisely, Tir Na Nog.

"That doesn't make sense," Mera argued. "Tir Na Nog is on the opposite side of the country."

"Also, most fae can't pop in here as they wish because of the barrier that protects Clifftown," Bast added. "Winnowing would be hard, but not impossible, I suppose."

Back in the twenties, there were enough random attacks

from revolutionary witches and fae to justify magical barriers around the human state. After all, humans had occupied the lowest levels of the Tagradian food chain for a long while before their technological boost. Before they joined the fight against the treacherous mermaids and helped the rest of the nation win.

Despite their aid, many supernaturals felt threatened by human technology. Though nowadays, the relations between the different states were amicable.

Still, the barriers around Clifftown stood.

Just in case.

"As far as I recall, most *pixies* have wings," Julian clarified, his tone oozing poison. "The killer could've drowned Sara Hyland, then flown with the body into Clifftown."

Bast shook his head. "The journey would take days, even if the killer didn't stop for food and water. We're magical creatures, human, but we're not one of your machines."

How had he managed to make "human" an insult?

Mera turned to Julian. "I hate to side with Bast on this one, but Sara had been dead for ten hours when we found her. There's no way the murderer could've flown from Tir Na Nog that quickly without teleportation. I mean *winnowing*," she corrected herself when Bast made a face.

"Whoever did this is either powerful enough to break through the barrier, or rich enough to pay someone who could," the Cap said. "Mera, I've booked tickets to Tir Na Nog for you both, and I've alerted your precinct, Detective Dhay. The two of you leave in the morning."

Julian eyed Bast with suspicion. "Cap, I should join them."

"I agree," Mera added, not caring to hide the smile she shot at her partner. The real one, that is, not the fae prick standing beside her.

"Negative." Ruth pointed at Julian. "I need you here providing support for Mera, and working Richard Hegway's case. But you'll keep her up to date with new findings regarding the crime scene or the bodies, understood?"

For a moment, he didn't say anything. Mera could swear he was about to oppose, but instead, Julian's shoulders slumped. "Yes, Cap."

"Good. Will you excuse us for a moment?"

With a frown, he glanced at Mera, then at the Cap again, as if to make sure he hadn't heard the order wrong. However, Julian knew better than to make the Cap repeat herself, so he nodded and left, closing the door behind him.

Ruth leaned back on her chair. "I've spoken to your Captain, Detective Dhay, and we agree that if you and Detective Maurea solve this case, we'd like to make your association permanent."

"Wait," Mera interrupted. "Permanent?"

The Cap nodded. "We want to use you as an example of unity between Hollowcliff's law enforcement. Encourage teamwork and communication between the different districts. God knows we need it, especially now that a fae died in human territory."

"No," Mera blurted. Noticing Bast's silence, she glanced back at him. "No. Right? I mean, you probably have a partner back in your precinct, and—"

"I work alone. No self-respecting fae wants a nightling for a partner."

Her heart broke a little at that. Her siren instinct urged her to hug him.

"Some have been brave enough to do it, mind you," he added, "but I quickly changed their minds."

Jerk.

The pity Mera had felt drained from her at once.

"Nothing for you to worry about, kitten." He gave her a cocky grin. "You're smarter than my previous partners, and I don't entirely detest you, so I suppose that's a plus."

Fuck that.

Half of Mera's weight rested on her palms as she leaned over Ruth's mahogany table. She kept her tone calm and gentle, hoping it would help. "Cap, Jules is my partner. He always has been. I'm not okay with this."

"Detective," she spoke with the tone of an approaching thunderstorm. "I never asked for your permission."

With that, the Cap turned back to the window and motioned for them to go.

CHAPTER 4

Somewhere in the past...

THE MOON SHONE fiercely in the clear night sky.

Mera walked out of the water, dragging a body with one hand by its russet hair with long curls—so similar to her own. In the other hand, she held a shovel she'd found inside a sunken ship.

Mera had been only a merling then. She hadn't gotten her bosoms like Belinda Tiderider yet, nor the elongated fins behind her ankles and on the edges of her ears, which denounced her coming of age. And yet, she'd defeated this warrior with a lifetime of experience and spite; this corpse that weighed a boulder of hate.

All to save her home, Atlantea.

The final battle had cost Mera everything, but it didn't matter now. She would be meeting her end soon.

The waves helped push them both to shore. Almost as if

the ocean encouraged her to see this through. Almost as if it thanked her.

The war corals protecting her body were broken and shattered. She threw away the pieces that hung on the shark-leather straps, and only her scaled bodysuit remained. It probably wouldn't serve its purpose of helping her walk on land, or breathe air with ease, since it had been ripped and torn beyond repair.

The change took over the minute she stepped out of the water.

Her fins sunk back into her body, disappearing from sight. Her thick, light-gray skin acquired a pearly hue, becoming softer as pores spread atop it.

The pull of what humans called gravity weighed on her at once. Mera dropped on her knees and vomited all the water in her lungs.

Clearly the bodysuit wasn't working.

Still, her grasp on those lifeless curls, and the shovel, didn't wane.

Once Mera could breathe, the air making a wheezing sound as it cut through her throat, she forced herself up and walked on. Her bones felt like broken glass, and she had to use the shovel's handle as a crutch to steady her steps. But she didn't stop.

Mera knew she would start feeling a tingling sensation soon. That's how those who crossed the forbidden zone described it—a tingling at first, then a growing burn that spread along your skin, pierced into your bones, and ate you whole until there was nothing left but ashes.

Few had managed to return to the safe zone in time, bearing severe burns and missing limbs. Most, however, simply crumbled onto themselves, puffing into nonexistence.

She dragged the body behind her, leaving a line on the sand.

Air burned Mera's lungs, her legs stung harder, and she wanted to give up, but Professor Currenter's lesson echoed in her ears.

"Walking comes rather instinctively, but breathing... Oh, younglings, it takes a while to get used to that. When we practice on the Isles of Fog, you'll see the difference between stepping on land, with and without a suit." Mera remembered the sorrow in his tone as he continued... *"None of said islands, however, will offer you a delicious stew."*

His wrinkled fins stretched wide as the old waterbreaker drew in water, which filtered out through the membranes in his neck, torso and legs. As if he could smell this thing called a stew.

"Cooked food, children. Thank Poseidon you'll never know what that is. Better than to spend the rest of your days craving for it."

Mera walked farther. Her pain⬛physical and emotional⬛ didn't matter. Neither did Professor Currenter; not anymore.

She dragged the body through the sand and into the edge of what had to be a forest, though it looked so different from the algae plantations she knew, and strangely, so similar.

Feeling the fluffy and moist soil underneath the palms of her feet, she stopped. Mera wiggled her toes against it and smiled.

Earth felt so different from sand. It still stuck to her soles, though.

On she went, propped by the upside-down shovel, until she found a clearing circled by bushes.

She let go of the body, spun the shovel to its correct position, and dug.

"This is how you bury a body," Professor Currenter had said, showing it to the class on an abandoned beach near the Isles of Fog, an unprotected archipelago near Atlantea. For the exercise, he'd used a piece of coral instead of a dead body,

which in retrospect, was quite wise. *"Those who commit the severest of offenses are buried on dry land, as has been our way for generations."*

Belinda, Mera's best friend, had raised her hand. *"Why is that?"*

He'd stopped shoveling and leaned on the tool. With his scaled bodysuit, the professor and the rest of the class had no problems with breathing or adapting to the harsher surface force he called gravity. *"Those buried on land can never be found by Poseidon on the day of Regneerik. Not that I believe in such things, but it's become a tradition that denounces great shame."*

Mera breathed faster from the effort, and the air hurt her lungs. Her muscles stung from the exertion of shoveling, but her movements were quicker than she'd expected.

Maybe a part of her bodysuit was still working.

Mother's voice echoed in her ears. *"One day, you'll know what's best for our people, weakling."*

Mera stopped to glance back at Queen Ariella's body. "Who knew you'd be right?"

Her mother didn't reply.

Tears went down Mera's cheeks as she kept digging. Her movements might be quick, but her body felt heavier with each passing second.

A little longer.

She was nearly done.

Once she was satisfied with the depth of the grave, she took the body by its ankle and dragged it into the hole. It made a hollow, wet sound. Then nothing.

She watched the lifeless queen below, her limbs twisted like broken twigs, her milky eyes glaring at Mera. Odd that the protective magic around Tagrad hadn't burnt the corpse into ashes. The spell probably didn't consider a dead water-breaker a threat.

Wondering why the magic hadn't started eating her alive, Mera patted her own body.

Soon it would, though. It had to.

She should probably hurry.

"I reject you and what you stand for," she proclaimed as she dug from the mound on her left back into the hole. Each word Professor Currenter had recited that day jumped to mind, as clear as the waters near the Islands of Fog. "May you stay here until Poseidon returns from the depths of the sea to bring reckoning upon every living creature. May you remain on land, hidden from his sight so he does not find you, so he does not call you to the fight. May you spend eternity in this grave, forever forgotten and in shame."

She spat into the hole, filling it with dirt while grieving tears strolled down her cheeks.

A smile cut through her lips, though.

Mera was free.

She would die, but she was free.

When she finished, she slammed the back of the shovel on the grave, once, twice. As if making sure her mother could never escape. Sealing the queen in her own disgrace.

She walked back to the beach and stopped at the edge of the water. Throwing the shovel into the waves, she screamed.

Her desperate cry of sorrow carried in the wind, for the friends and family she'd lost. For the home that was forever gone.

She was tired, so very tired, and still she screamed for all the things she'd done; horrid things the grownups from Atlantea had refused to do. Unspeakable things; unforgivable things.

Yes, Mera was just a merling, but her childhood had ended today because of them. Because of her mother, too.

She had saved her people from the mad queen. That had

to count for something, and yet, right here, alone and exiled, forgotten underneath the stars, it didn't.

At all.

Mera fell with her knees on the sand as her legs caved.

Her broken song of sorrow kept bursting from her lips, rippling along the water's surface, until Mera's throat felt like raw flesh, and even then, she kept screaming, aching for the ocean to which she could never return, mourning for her own life; the life she'd lost.

The life she never had.

She released one final howl of defeat, so frail it came out as a whimper.

Her end could come now. She was ready.

Where was the magic that would consume her in scorching agony? The pain in her bones and flesh had waned. They said the lack of feeling always preceded the end, that it meant death had taken your hand.

Mera welcomed death's touch. She couldn't keep breathing after everything she'd gone through. Her short, miserable existence had to end, please, Gods above and below, she couldn't take it anymore.

"Poseidon in the trenches," she begged as she stared into the waves, her voice merely a whisper, "take my soul into its never-ending sleep."

But he never did.

CHAPTER 5

MERA DROPPED her duffel bag on the floor and leaned on the ticket counter. "I'm here to pick up my tickets for the Tir Na Nog Express at three o'clock." She pushed her ID forward.

The faerie behind the glass, a banshee with oily hair, pale skin, and dark circles around her eyes, took the ID and typed something on the computer. She handed the document back to Mera, watching her with cold indifference. *"Ae hak'le finuest. Wu kar mit fae wahnala, pesut."*

Pesut. *Human.* One of two words she knew in Faeish.

As long as the banshee didn't call her *akritana*—literal translation: waterbreaker—Mera was damn fine with being a *pesut*.

"Lady, my Faeish sucks."

The banshee rolled her milky irises and pointed to a sign on the wall behind her that read, *"Humans must present a written certificate from the Tir Na Nog border agency, or have a fae citizen vouch for them."*

"That's stupid. Tir Na Nog is a borough of Hollowcliff! There shouldn't be a border agency in the first place."

"I do not make rules," the banshee argued with a heavy accent.

"And I don't give a rat's—"

"She's just doing her job, kitten." Bast appeared beside Mera.

He flashed the banshee a charming grin that could turn any female's knees into jelly. *"Felenue, ae kachst mat, kuata."*

The banshee smiled rows of razor-sharp teeth that reminded Mera of a shark. She printed two tickets, stamped them, and handed them to Bast.

"Kitas," he offered, before walking away.

Grabbing her bag, Mera followed him. "Hey, are you giving me my ticket?"

He stopped and turned so abruptly, that she nearly slammed nose-first against his chest. He held the tickets a little too high. "Here you go."

Ha, tough luck for him. Mera could stand on the tips of her toes like any human—a skill that had taken her a while to master. She snatched her ticket and searched for the big screen that showed the departures and their platforms.

A metallic scent suddenly invaded her nostrils. It was that same magic she'd felt back at UCH. Again, it flickered in and out of range, as if it was trying to hide but failing miserably.

Mera glanced around, scanning for any supernaturals she could find, but the scent hadn't come from the group of soccer-mom witches on the left—their magic smelled like strawberries—or the two beefy bloodsucking "bros" who caught her eye, and thought she was flirting with them— theirs was weak and smelled like rotting blood.

"That's your type?" Bast asked from behind, his breath tickling the curve of her neck. "I thought it was human, blonde, and dumb."

Mera swiveled on her heels, ready to give him a serious lesson on personal boundaries, but Poseidon in the trenches!

He was standing too close. She stared at him, her heart slamming against her ribcage nonstop until she had the courage to step back.

It was either that or having a heart attack.

"First, my type is none of your business," she warned. "Second, I need coffee, and third, did you find our platform yet?"

"Forty-five A." He nodded to a nearby coffee stall. "Come on, then. I enjoy coffee as much as any human. Genius concoction, really."

Clutching the handle of her bag, she followed him, trying to ignore how swiftly he moved underneath that perfectly fitted shirt, and how broad and strong his shoulders were.

Poseidon help her, his butt… her siren urges wanted to bite it or squeeze it. Actually, both.

Mera forced herself to look away as Bast ordered their coffees, noticing how most people glared at him—with a mix of hate and disgust, some with annoyance. It was strange seeing those who had openly accepted her refuse him so heatedly.

Well, they'd only accepted Mera because they thought she was human. If they'd known she was a siren…

'Waterbreaker,' the ravenous force inside her whispered. *'You're not human, so stop thinking like one. Siren. Mermaid. You're not these names they have for you.'*

Shut up, she told herself.

'Waterbreaker. Atlantean. Queen. That's who you are.'

"You have to act and think like one of us," the Cap's voice burst in her mind. *"Condition yourself to be human in order to become human."*

So, she did.

Nowadays, Mera felt more human than siren. Most of the time, at least.

Bast soon returned with two beige plastic cups with

white covers. Mera could smell his roast blend from a mile away. "You prefer your coffee bitter and dark."

"Like my soul, kitten." He winked at her as he handed over her cup. "You have a strong sense of smell for a human."

"Genetics," she muttered as she busied herself with drinking her mocha.

He took a sip of his own coffee, then observed the clock hanging from the station's ceiling. "We should head to the platform."

When they arrived, a black train shaped like a bullet waited for them. It didn't follow the pattern from the regional trains to the other boroughs—those were white with a red line cutting through their length.

"The hull is made of carbon fiber. Everything has iron in the human world, including the paint you use on your trains." Bast explained, seeing the question on her face.

Pure iron cancelled magic. It was why fae and witches hated technology, even though most things nowadays were made of steel alloys that had nearly no trace of the element. Iron didn't affect shifters and vamps at all, though, so they loved technology as much as humans did. In fact, Lycannie was a major hub for hackers.

"Isn't it just pure iron that hurts you?"

"Yes, but we don't trust your devices anyway." He nodded to the train. "Your paint might not steal our powers, but we're a superstitious kind."

"That's silly. Tagrad does everything it can to include you. It's why products made of pure iron are forbidden, including here in the human borough. Well, except for iron handcuffs, but those are kept for special cases."

He shrugged, and that was his only argument.

Only then did she notice that Bast didn't carry any guns.

She patted hers, which was attached to her belt, while a dagger hung from the opposite side in its sheath. Mera sighed in relief. A Clifftown detective needed a gun, or he'd be dead during his first month on duty. Mera's own weapon had saved her life more times than she could count.

"Is your distaste for iron the reason why you don't carry guns?" she asked.

"Not exactly. I've never been a fan of firearms," he said simply. "Plus, they're not a requirement in my precinct."

"How about swords or daggers?" she pushed. "They're made of bronze or carbon. Lots of faeries use them and so could you."

"I could, yes."

But he didn't.

"Seriously, Bast," she huffed in frustration. "How do you defend yourself?"

He wiggled his fingers. "Magic." Yet, magic was so diverse, so mutable in its nature, that no answer might've been better.

As soon as they stepped inside the train, the carts began moving sluggishly across the tracks.

The inside was made of polished mahogany with swirly golden details attached to the surface. The scent of pine coursed through the corridor, and ornate wall lights hung in the space between the windows. This décor vastly differed from the train's sleek and modern hull, but most Sidhe loved this type of decadent-royal vibe.

She and Bast walked past mostly empty cabins. Some were filled with merchants and their goods. Others, with men in expensive suits—she guessed politicians—while other cabins had groups of women, all of them young and pretty. Some handsome men, too.

'They do what the fae won't,' her siren whispered.

The light courts forbade intercourse with humans, even if that went against the Agreement of Cordiality. Zev Ferris' murder must've been a big middle finger to those racist jerks, especially considering Sara Hyland was carrying his child.

It was not like faeries didn't break their own law, though. These men and women were in this train, probably because of a horny fae in a high-up place who enjoyed the thrill.

As they passed one of the cabins, a group of women wearing bright colors and short skirts called to Bast. He winked at them, then tilted his head as if tipping an invisible hat.

"Ladies," he greeted, before continuing on his way.

A pang of annoyance prickled Mera's chest, but she couldn't imagine why she felt this way.

He led her to a small cabin with two long padded seats that could pass for beds. Their red velvet surface seemed comfortable and luxurious. The seats faced each other, both with pillows resting near the windows.

Bast placed his duffel bag below the right seat, and Mera pushed hers underneath the left one. She took off her leather jacket and hung it on a small coat rack that was attached to a thin strip of wall next to the cabin's door.

Sitting down, she put her coffee atop the small table between their seats, and fixed her hair up into a high pony-tail. A few russet threads escaped the rubber band and curled over her collarbone.

Across from her, Bast sat, staring at the spot. His focus drifted up toward her chin, landing on her lips. He crossed his legs, as if putting a barrier between them—apparently the table wasn't enough.

His burning gaze didn't leave her, however, and Mera would have given anything to find out what he was thinking.

'He likes what he sees,' her siren whispered.

"So, do you have wings?" she asked in a pitiful attempt at making small talk.

He blinked out of his trance and set his coffee next to hers. "I might have."

"Come on. You can't give me one straight answer?" She shook her head. "Some partner you are."

"Fine. Yes, I have wings." He looked out the window. Buildings and streets passed by in a blur of concrete and sharp squares.

Mera narrowed her eyes at him. "Are you sure?"

"They're hidden by magic." He chuckled. "You amuse me, kitten."

"Glad to be of service," she grumbled as she observed the rushing landscape. "It's weird that our capital is divided into five boroughs so far from one another, isn't it?"

He took a sip of his coffee. "I think the distance is what keeps us united. Can you imagine shifters, vampires, witches, fae, and humans crammed into one place? We'd have a war within days." He was undoubtedly, and absolutely, right. "Besides, fae enjoy keeping to themselves."

"Yeah," she snorted. "I heard about the inbreeding in royal houses."

He raised one finger. "That only happens in the light fae courts. Winter and Night are much more diverse, I assure you," he explained as if he was defending his honor. After taking a last gulp of his coffee, Bast slammed the empty cup on the table. "How about we get to know each other?"

She frowned. "Why?"

"If we solve this case, we might become long-term partners. And I don't know much about you. So…"

"Julian is my official partner, and he'll keep his position once we're done, I assure you." Crossing her arms, she leaned back on her padded seat. "Besides, who said I want to get to know you?"

"Everyone does." He showed her his face and dashing smile as if that was enough, and damned the old gods, her siren agreed. "You do too, kitten. You just don't say it."

She snorted but was actually terrified. He'd read right through her, and if he could see that…

"Let's play a game," he added, leaning his elbow on the windowsill. "I'll tell you something about you, and you'll tell me something about me. Whoever is wrong will owe the other a favor."

"That sounds awfully like a deal."

Everyone knew the golden rule: never make deals with a fae.

"Come on. It will be fun." He drew an X on his chest with his thumb. "I promise no mischief. What do you say?"

She already hated this pointless game, but they didn't have anything better to do for the next day. Plus, getting a favor from a faerie could eventually come in handy.

"Okay," she gave in. "You start."

Bast hunched over his knees and stared at her. "You have a secret."

She didn't hesitate. "Everyone does."

"Oh, it's a big, juicy one!" Delight invaded his face. "And it's not the fact you're desperately in love with that partner of yours. That's too obvious."

An infuriating warmth rose to her cheeks. "I'm not in love with Jules!"

'Liar, liar, pants on fire,' her siren crooned.

"Please, don't embarrass yourself, kitten. No, it's something else." He tapped his knees and leaned back. "I'll find out what it is, sooner or later."

'Be my fucking guest,' her siren countered through gritted teeth, no longer flirtatious and swooning, but hungry for blood.

"Oh yeah, how about you?" Mera pushed. "You are from high birth."

The more Mera interacted with him, the more she saw it. It was the way he used informal speech to hide it, the way he moved, and how offended he'd gotten when she'd mentioned royal inbreeding.

Sure, Bast was night fae, but kind-of-banished royalty was still royalty. She knew that better than anyone.

His eyes widened and he smiled. "I might be."

"Which begs the question, why are you a detective? Why not eat and fuck your wealth away?"

He watched her for a moment, his blue gaze piercing through her. It made Mera uncomfortable and her siren happy at the same time.

"I suppose I lacked purpose," he finally admitted, his tone heavy and yet alluring. "So, I enlisted."

Mera's instincts told her this wasn't the whole truth; that there was a mountain of things he kept from her.

"My turn," he cooed. "You don't let people in easily."

"Neither do you." She studied him carefully, her fingers tapping on the table. "There's darkness inside you, Sebastian Dhay."

It was a stupid statement considering he was a nightling, and yet, it hit Bast with the strength of a punch to the gut. The amusement in his eyes vanished, quickly replaced by a deep sadness.

He cleared his throat as he watched his own hands. "Don't we all have darkness inside us?"

Yes, but not like his. Not like hers, either.

Better not to push.

"You're right," she conceded.

She watched the building blocks and chaos of the city wane into endless grass fields, revealing a peaceful and sunny countryside.

The train crossed a few small towns, stopping at a shifter village called Wulfham. As far as Mera could see, no one boarded.

"Wolves hate us more than humans do," Bast answered

her unspoken question, and then they were moving again. "Other shifters are usually less... temperamental."

"Temperamental? You openly call werewolves mutts. Of course they hate you."

A certain anger swirled behind his irises. "I have never, and will never, call a werewolf a mutt. Understand?"

Oh, she'd struck a nerve.

Mera 1, Bast 0.

"Fine. But you can't deny the fact that most fae are snob-bish assholes, and that's why everyone hates you all." She took the last sip of her mocha and nearly spat it out—it had gone cold.

"You're right. I can't." Something glinted in his eyes, but before Mera had time to wonder what it might be, he turned to the window and watched the passing scenery.

"Your borough is the most corrupt in Hollowcliff," she said. A fact rather than an assumption.

Bast ignored her.

"I know it's because royal Sidhe refuse to abide by Tagra-dian law. They think they're more than the rest of us," she pushed. "It's not your district's fault, by the way. I get that."

"You do?" He raised his brow.

"You can't fully enforce the law and keep the peace with the courts at the same time. Which is why you get *carte blanche* on a lot of matters. Avoiding civil war comes before following the law."

"Your point?"

"You're a royal Sidhe working as a detective."

His nostrils flared as he glared at her. "I'll pretend you didn't just accuse me of corruption."

"That's not what—"

"Mera." His lips formed a thin line. A mix of outrage and fury burned behind his eyes.

She watched his profile, all sharp, squared lines; then the

slight hollow between his jaw and cheekbones that became evident when he swallowed. Strands of loose hair hung above his temples like threads of starlight. Even in his anger, Bast was beautifully sad. And this sorrow inside him, this hurt, it somehow resonated with Mera's own.

"Your game sucked," she grumbled.

"Yes, it did."

The train halted abruptly and Bast nearly slammed into her. He'd been fast enough to stop before the table, but his upper body arched over it and he'd nearly pinned Mera against her seat.

"Hey, watch it!"

He looked down, shooting her a bewildered grin. The loose strands of his silver hair making him resemble a madman. "Can you feel it?"

Magic. Sizzling, boiling, magic. With a metallic taste.

Whoever had been following them had come out to play.

"What are you talking about?" she lied, because as far as Bast could tell she was human, and humans couldn't sense magic.

This magic wasn't similar to Bast's, though. It was more chaotic, less stable.

Witch magic.

The metal in the carts groaned loudly before the entire train boosted up, then stopped. For a split second, Mera was weightless. It felt like floating in a current, letting the ocean take her where it wanted.

She drifted midair along with Bast, their suitcases, and the shards of glass from the broken window as the metal twisted around them.

Reaching out for her, he pulled Mera to him, cocooning her with his body.

Was he protecting her?

He thought she was human, so yes. He was. Which made Mera feel terribly guilty for implying he might be corrupt.

The warmth of his skin irradiated into her as the train dropped with fury. They crashed to the ground with a violent shrieking boom, the screech of metal bursting around them.

Bast groaned, and Mera immediately freed from his grasp. "Are you okay?" She checked him for broken ribs or limbs, but he seemed fine.

He winced. "I've been worse."

Fury swirled inside her, a type of rage she hadn't felt in a long time. The same type that had killed her mother.

Peeking out of the glassless window, she spotted a hooded figure standing a few carts ahead in front of the train.

"Come out from wherever you are, detectives!" the figure yelled.

Bast swayed as he forced himself to stand. Once he balanced on his feet, he straightened his posture and pulled down the edges of his gray vest. He wiped away the shards of broken glass that peppered his white shirt, then watched the hooded figure who had just upended an entire train.

"Look at that, kitten. We have company."

CHAPTER 6

FAN-FUCKING-TASTIC.

As a detective in the human borough, pretending to be a human, Mera wouldn't be able to use her powers. Sure, she had spelled people into telling the truth, but a siren's song could be like a toned-down version of a vamp's glamour, so it usually went under the radar.

However, to fight a witch who could lift an eight-ton train as if it were made of paper, she would need more. Much more.

The macabre.

No. Not that. Never that.

Maybe Mera could do this old school. After all, supernaturals bled just like humans.

Back in Clifftown, she'd often faced misbehaving vamps and shifters. A stake to the heart or a silver bullet had been more than enough, but bloodsuckers and morphs had close to no magic in them.

Witches and warlocks? Totally different ballgame.

They were humans with a talent for magic, which was enhanced by the runes they tattooed over their bodies.

Evanorians might not be as powerful as faeries, but they got damn close.

Exchanging a knowing glance with Bast, Mera tapped the gun holster attached to the left side of her belt, then the dagger sheathed on the right, and hoped they would be enough.

As she and her *temporary* partner stepped out of the train and walked ahead, she noticed he had a mad glint in his eyes, which matched the slight grin on his face. It was as if a bewildered force—or presence—both beautiful and terrifying had taken over him.

He also seemed utterly unafraid of the witch who had come for them.

"Bast? You okay?"

"Never better." He didn't turn to her, his gaze fixed on the hooded figure standing ahead.

A long dirt patch followed the train tracks. Left and right, endless green prairies unfurled toward the horizon.

People slowly got out from the crumpled wreckage, and Mera spotted the groups of escorts, businessmen, and merchants helping each other. A warm sensation spread in her chest. From what she could gather, most passengers were injured but not badly. Some limped while others supported them, but most could walk on their own.

When they spotted the witch ahead, they gasped and ran as fast as they could. They clearly knew what witches could do, specially one who had levelled an entire train.

Mera and Bast stopped at a safe distance from their opponent. She couldn't see the witch's face from underneath the hood. The woman was completely clad in a black robe with a silver insignia shaped like a firebird. A belt riddled with weapons hung around her waist.

"Were you following us before?" Mera asked.

The witch nodded.

"What do you want?"

She pointed at Bast, displaying a swirling ink that decorated her skin up to her fingers. "It has been foreseen that you'll be *his* doom. Therefore, you must die, Sebastian Dhay." The witch craned her neck at Mera. "You may leave, human."

"The fuck I will," Pulling her gun from the holster, she removed the safety and aimed.

The witch laughed, leaning back slightly, and Bast screamed for Mera, but it was too late.

As the witch bent forward, a wave of magic burst from her body; a tsunami of wild energy ready to crush her and Bast. The magic's yellow flares cut the air toward them so fast, that Mera didn't have time to pull the trigger.

The blast threw them both on the ground.

All breath left Mera's lungs when her back slammed against the dirt. She closed her fingers around thin air— where her gun should have been—but it had slipped from her hand, landing some eight feet away.

Fucking witches.

"Stay down, kitten," Bast ordered as he jumped to his feet and closed his fists.

Darkness swam down his elbows, enveloping his lower arms and hands into a void, almost as if a part of Bast was made by the deepest night Mera had ever seen.

The darkness spread up from his skin, enveloping him in a black aura. Maybe Mera had lost her mind, but she could spot tiny stars twinkling in the void.

At the sight, the witch swallowed dry, but didn't hesitate. "Captionem!"

Bast's arms snapped toward his torso as if an invisible viper had wrapped around him. His angry void writhed like a caged animal, the same way Bast did. He pushed against the magic but couldn't break free.

His bun fell loose from the effort, freeing his long, moonlight-silver hair. His eyes widened with shock. "How's a witch—"

She took a pendant from underneath her robe and showed it to him; a golden hexagon with a red ruby attached to the middle.

Power enhancers.

Mera had heard about them, but never actually seen one since they were illegal.

"Ah, so you're cheating," Bast snarled as he fought to break free. "Seems hardly fair. The runes inked on your body should've given you enough advantage."

"I know who I'm up against." The witch put the pendant back underneath the fabric. "Besides, assassins and bounty hunters never play fair. Don't you recognize my insignia?" She pointed to the silver bird stamped on her robe.

Bast stopped fighting against the invisible grip, his chest heaving. "House Fillanmore," he grumbled.

No way.

House Fillanmore was an urban legend. Mercenary witches hired for hits on important people. They made the job look like an accident or a death by natural causes, which was why law enforcement assumed claims of their existence were just stories. If a death looked and smelled like a heart attack or a suicide, it usually was exactly that.

In most cases.

Mera glanced back at the crumpled train. House Fillanmore's supposed discretion was definitely out of the window.

The witch stepped closer to Bast, her movements sinuous and fluid.

Good. As long as she was distracted with him, she wouldn't notice Mera crawling toward her gun.

The mercenary removed a dagger from the belt around her robe. It had a curvy yet sharp blade, and the silver handle was encrusted with red emeralds. "Killing you will not bring me joy, sweet prince." She raised the dagger and ran the blade's belly down his cheek. "You're a fine specimen of your kind."

"You have no fucking clue," he grumbled before a black wave of energy burst from his core, flinging the witch away and cutting the air above Mera's head.

Bast's eyes went fully black as flaming night—that was the only way to describe it—bloomed from his fists.

He grinned, and Mera could swear his canines had grown sharper.

The witch stood up, blood trickling down her forehead. The impact had pushed her hood back to reveal a girl with lush red hair and tribal tattoos over her face and neck. She couldn't be much older than eighteen, but witches loved a good old magic facelift.

Considering the strength of her attacks, this one must be fifteen going on one hundred.

Mera finally reached her gun and stood up, aiming at the witch's head. "Stop!" She ordered. "You're under arrest!"

"Your bullets are worthless, human," she snapped.

Wrong. Mera had packed special bullets with the Cap's approval. These babies were granted on special inter-borough missions. Mera wouldn't waltz in Tir Na Nog with normal weaponry. She wasn't stupid.

"These bullets are made of iron. They might not stop you completely, but they will cut through any magic shield you create." She shrugged. "Through your flesh and bone, too."

The witch cursed Mera under her breath but made no sign to attack. Instead, she raised her hands slowly in surrender.

Bast glared at Mera with those beastly eyes and snarled, as if he were a wild animal and she'd stolen his prey.

"Bast?"

"The honor to kill should be mine." He stepped closer, ready to attack her.

She kept her aim at the witch but wondered if she should pivot the gun toward her new partner. "Bast, what the hell are you doing?"

Shaking his head, he halted. His eyes turned blue again and the whipping tentacles of night over his fists disappeared. He blinked at Mera and straightened his stance, once again the fae she knew.

"I'm sorry," he said, his tone strained. "Good job."

She would have to ask him about this night-flaming-demon shenanigan later. They had more pressing concerns right now.

Glancing away, she focused on the witch. "I thought house Fillanmore was known for their discretion," Mera nodded to the crumpled train behind her. "What changed?"

"I wanted to take my new pendant for a test run," she explained simply, eyeing Bast as he approached with a pair of cuffs in his hand. "Our leader approved."

"Yeah? And who hired you?" Mera pressed.

"Humans," the woman spat with disgust. "You think you're so powerful with your gadgets, but you're all so ignorant."

Mera sensed the wave of magic swirling inside the witch. "Don't even think about—"

"Captionem!"

The magic was faster than a thought. Mera fired but missed the witch's head by an inch. Her gun clanked on the ground, and she tried to pick it up, but her body didn't move.

Mera floated a few steps above the earth, trapped in the air. "Bitch!" she spat as magic twirled around her and squeezed.

Bast grumbled under his breath, a shield of night and

stars standing between him and the witch. That's why the magic hadn't worked on him.

He certainly learned his lessons.

The redhead shook her index finger left and right at Mera. "Time to let the grownups play, human."

Bast's shield vanished into thin air. Licking his lips, he threw the cuffs on the ground. "I suppose an arrest isn't an option here?"

"Either you die, or I do."

"I see." He and the witch began walking in circles like two beasts about to prowl. "How much did they pay you, red?"

"A hundred thousand coins."

"That's a lot. I'll double that if you give me the name of the person who wants me dead."

"Don't you see my house's emblem, *pixie*?" She tapped the insignia across her chest.

"Ah, so your famous code of honor isn't as flexible as your discretion."

The assassin smiled as yellow neon flares that smelled like watermelon spun around her, enveloping her body in three cutting rings of magic.

"You know, that's an oxymoron," Mera noted from her invisible prison, not bothering to try and break free—she knew she couldn't. "Bounty hunters have no honor."

"It's why house Fillanmore's prices are exorbitant," Bast countered as night flames sprouted from his skin and his eyes became beady-black again. "They rarely go back on a bounty."

The outer side of the yellow rings morphed into several pointy shapes, and in one impulse, the witch flung them toward Bast and Mera. The magic daggers swarmed upon them.

"Too easy." Bast chuckled.

A cloud of night shot from his hands, ripping through the air, and sucked the daggers into a void.

All except one.

It pierced through Bast's night and hit Mera in her stomach, a hot poker that slammed right through her.

Motherfucker, it hurt!

She held the screams that pushed out, but tears coursed down her cheeks anyway. The magic burned inside her gut, hissing and merciless. The assassin must've used the necklace's power to make one invincible dagger for Bast. It missed its target and hit Mera, though.

Tough luck.

The magic trapping her dwindled, and Mera fell to the ground. The dagger lodged in her entrails vanished into thin air, and blood began flowing from the wound.

"*Sakala wu, baku!*" Bast screamed, his fangs sharpening.

Baku. It meant something bad, but Mera couldn't remember what. She should have, since cursing had been the only interesting part of her school lessons in Faeish.

Sakala wu, on the other hand, had been much easier to remember. It meant "Fuck you."

Mera spotted a deep cut on the upper side of his right arm. His white shirt soaked up the intense wine-red⬛a little darker than normal blood⬛that flowed from the wound, but Bast didn't seem to notice.

So, the witch had created two deadly daggers, but only one had hit the target.

A storm of rumbling darkness rose from Bast's body, thunder cracking inside a cumulus of void and stars without any lightning. It was magnificent and terrifying to watch.

The witch's eyes turned fully white as a shield spread around her, protecting her from the surge of night that crashed upon her, swallowing the grass, trees, and even the train tracks ahead.

When the darkness receded, there was nothing but death in its wake. The metal in the tracks had corroded, nearby trees were left leafless and curling as if swallowed by a merciless fire, and black ashes covered the space green grass had occupied a moment ago.

The witch's shield had protected her from the surge, though her skin looked reddish, and her fingers were dark with something that resembled frostbite.

Bast didn't wait. He ran at her, punching through the shield. It shattered the way crystal breaks.

He jabbed her stomach with his blazing void, burning through her robe. The witch howled in pain but managed to cut a line over his chest with one of the daggers from her belt.

With one quick, mighty blast, she flung Bast away, slamming him straight into the train's face.

The metal groaned as his body pierced a dent in it. He fell unconscious to the ground.

"Bast…" Mera stretched her hand toward him. She tried to stand up, but the pain from the wound spread across her body, rendering her useless and whimpering.

"I must be quick," the witch said mostly to herself, a certain fear in her tone as she hurried toward Bast, unsheathing yet another of her daggers.

"Please don't hurt him," Mera begged through gritted teeth.

A gut wound was fatal. Not only that, but it would be a slow, agonizing death, and there were no hospitals nearby.

I die on land. Like any other human…

The thought brought her a certain peace.

The witch stopped in her tracks and came to Mera. She peeked at the wound, then opened her hand. Sharp yellow rings spun around her wrist. "I'll make it quick."

A part of Mera wanted to take the offer, appreciating her

mercy. Another part, however, remembered Bast would be next. It might be too late for Mera, but she wouldn't let someone else die because of this bitch.

She released her siren at once. The power coursed through her veins, swimming, singing, wanting. Hungry, thirsty, aching.

It connected to the witch—to her blood, to her muscles, and to the water in her tear ducts, to the bile in her stomach, and to the piss in her bladder.

The witch's eyes widened when she realized she couldn't move.

Mera pushed the macabre forward, and blood rushed through the woman's veins, nearly bursting the walls of her arteries.

Water was everywhere—in droplets in the sky, in rivers and oceans, even inside the earth. Inside every creature's body, too, and that was the terrible beauty of the macabre.

Mera's thoughts became dizzying, but she had to see this through till the end.

The magic in the witch's blood writhed against her control, but it was useless. No magic had ever won against the dance of death. This wasn't simple waterbending.

It was much, much more.

Controlling her, Mera made the witch lower her arm. She fought against it, but the more she did, the more her veins smashed against her muscles and bones, the more her capillary snapped, until her opponent surrendered with a painful yelp.

Mera built momentum inside the witch, using the blood in her veins and her heart, inside everything her flesh coated, until a storm thrashed within the woman's body.

The assassin trembled as tears tracked down her swollen cheeks, going down her chin, only to drift up into the air, floating around her.

"N-not like this," the woman begged. "Please. Not like this."

In that moment a pair of strong, tanned arms circled the witch's jaw and collar from behind. With one quick twist, they cracked her neck with a sound awfully similar to snapping branches.

The witch fell lifeless to the ground, revealing Bast standing behind her, his teeth gritted behind a curtain of moon-silver hair, along with his bewildered pitch-black eyes.

Mera pushed her siren essence back into her core, sighing in relief. She hadn't used the macabre, not to its full extent.

Thank Poseidon.

Coughing, she glanced down at the wound. It was soaked with her own blood, which flowed from the cut and pooled on the dirt.

Bast kneeled next to her, checking the wound, his eyes now blue and normal, but there was fear in them. Guilt, too.

"This doesn't look good, kitten." His tone was low and mournful.

Had he seen what she could do? Had he found out about her secret?

Did it matter?

She glanced down at her wound again. *Fuck, that was a lot of blood.* On the upside, she'd be losing consciousness soon. She could barely feel the pain anymore.

"Bast, it's okay," she assured, her voice weaker than she'd intended. "You did what you could."

He cupped her cheek, his eyes glistening. "I'll fix this. I promise."

Turning to the fields behind the train, Mera smiled. The sun shone from an impeccable blue sky, and birds chirped in the distance.

"It's peaceful…"

"You're not dying today, Detective," Bast snarled as he

took her in his arms and stood. He winced in pain because his right arm was wounded, but he didn't let go.

Mera rested her head on his shoulder, her body feeling too light. "You'll get blood on your fancy clothes," she whispered drowsily, "*pixie.*"

He chuckled as his arms tightened around her. "Hold on."

"Bast, you can't walk me to the next town," she insisted, her tone so frail she thought the words might break midway. "There's not enough time."

He arched an eyebrow at her. "Who said anything about walking?"

Wings sprouted from his back, silver draconian wings as smooth as a pearl, as smooth as his hair. Mera lost a breath as they spread wide, spanning at least two cars' width.

"You look like a water dragon."

She smiled at the memory, when she'd seen one cutting through water with her friends from school. The creature had no scales, its light-silver skin as thick as that of whales, as it dashed into the deep blue.

Legend said they were children of the moon and the stars. She couldn't tell if she thought about Bast or the dragon.

Maybe both.

A certain dizziness took over Mera when a surge of wind pushed down on her. Bast held her closer as she watched the ground shrink down below. Up ahead, the deep sapphire of the sky engulfed them.

Mera was flying. It seemed pretty amazing, and she should've been more excited, but her thoughts couldn't properly connect.

They boosted into the air, Bast's grip on her overly tight. Her partner was staring ahead, his silver hair swinging madly around him.

A beautiful water dragon.

'Waterbreaker, you're losing your mind.' her siren whispered.

She inhaled the woodsy scent at Bast's collar. "Not a bad way to go at all."

"Mera!" Bast called from what seemed to be a long distance. He shook her, but then she couldn't feel him near her anymore. "Mera!"

Everything went dark.

CHAPTER 7

Mera's russet hair floated around her as she bounced gently amidst the endless blue. She wiggled her ears, and her two, green side-fins wiggled along. Looking down at her pearly skin with sea-green scales on the edges, she grinned.

She was back! Poseidon in the trenches, she was home!

She boosted through rushing currents, free like she hadn't felt in a long time. An Orca whale swam above, trying to keep up with her pace, but Mera was a waterbreaker, and they had that name for a reason.

Thrusting forward, faster than the current itself, she quickly left the whale behind. She then took a turn and jolted toward the sky, breaking through the surface and looping in the air before diving back. She repeated the moves as she swam, once, twice, and soon dolphins followed her lead as the faint orange of sunset bathed the surface.

Once done with playtime, Mera plummeted toward the sea floor, swirling in her axis as she went.

Now that she was back, she would never leave, no matter what. But where should she go?

She couldn't return to Atlantea.

Queen Mera Wavestorm, savior of all merfolk, traitor to the throne, murderer of her own mother.

Tears pooled in her eyes, but the water washed them away. None of that mattered now. Mera's only wish, her only need, was to keep swimming.

Besides, the ocean was vast.

She halted near the sandy bottom, and spotted a dark form looming ahead. She swam closer to find a sunken frigate crashed on the sea floor. The ripped sail floated with the currents, as if the wind blew on it.

Jackpot! Mera loved exploring sunken ships.

Landriders owned the oddest things. Professor Currenter would eagerly go through the spoils she found, especially if there was any cutlery—he loved forks, perhaps because they resembled tiny tritons.

She boosted toward the ship, but slowed down when she found someone floating in her way. A female with navy fins and scales peppering the edges of her light-gray body.

The woman wore an armor of white shells and red corals that covered her breasts, waist, and knees. Her scaled bodysuit was the color of blood, and a tattered cape floated around her waist. Curly russet hair turned bright red where the faint sunlight hit it.

Mera shook her head, her chest squeezing. "No, no, no."

The woman smiled, her glassy green eyes shining with malice.

"You can't escape fate, daughter," she rasped with a dry, croaking voice that belonged to a decaying corpse.

Purple and black magic began eating away her mother, and when it vanished, the magic left a rotten carcass in its place.

Mother's tongue poked out from her left cheek, slithering between the two tendons that connected her cheekbone to her jaw. The queen's ribcage showed underneath her ripped bodysuit and tattered armor.

"You're not real," Mera told herself, fear and dread thrashing inside her.

The rotting skin and muscles below the corpse's left elbow had vanished, displaying her bones. Mother's perky nose was gone, replaced by two slits, and an empty socket gaped at Mera instead of her left eye.

The dead queen pointed a bony finger at her, smiling with brown teeth. "I'll see you in Regneerik, weakling."

Mera shrieked so loudly that the sea floor shook.

Suddenly, she wasn't underwater anymore. She stood near a beach, watching it from the shoreface, while her feet sunk slightly into the sandy floor. Hilarious really, that some landriders believed her people had fish tails, as if waterbreakers weren't children of both land and sea.

Up above, the moon shone behind sluggish clouds.

A nightmare. It had been a nightmare.

Mera steadied her breathing, coming to grips with where she was.

It was peaceful here, and the temperature quite pleasant—then again, waterbreakers adapted to extreme colds and squeezing pressures, so Mera wasn't exactly picky.

Standing on the sandy beach, a landrider watched her.

She should've been scared, but instead, she looked down at her body and the smooth skin that shone a glittering turquoise where moonlight struck. The long curls of her hair cascaded down her breasts, which had grown considerably.

Mera didn't have nipples or body hair, but she could swear she'd had them for the past thirteen years... Never mind. She was waterbreaker once again. And a full-grown female.

With full-grown female urges.

Mera rejoiced in the landrider's attention.

Her mother always enjoyed the flesh offerings from the tribes inhabiting the Isles of Fog. Why shouldn't Mera?

She stepped forward, her hips making slow, circular moves on the water. The waves brushed past her knees now.

The landrider stepped closer. His long hair was white, the rest of him hidden by darkness, but moonlight defined his sculpted chest and torso. His blue eyes were lighthouses that cut through the dark.

Magnificent.

He was naked, like her.

Hmm, Mera wanted to feast... in more ways than one.

Opening her mouth, she began singing. A sweet lullaby about tides and lost lovers that ensnared the male. She could see it by the way he'd begun moving, hurriedly and desperate.

He broke through the waves, unstoppable, hungry for her.

Oh, he was strong...

Soon he would reach Mera, and they would mate fiercely under the stars. She could feel him throbbing for her as much as she ached for him.

Mera couldn't wait. Landriders didn't have retractable genitals, and she was curious to see one for the first time.

'We've seen plenty since we've gotten to Clifftown,' a part of her whispered. 'Wake up!'

Mera shook her head. Was she losing her mind?

What was Clifftown?

It didn't matter. She and the male were about to mate. Once she screamed her release away and he came inside her...

Professor Currenter had once said cooked meals were divine. Mera couldn't remember trying a cooked meal, though a part of her whispered that's all she'd had for over a decade, except for that time when she ate sushi. It was the same part that said she wasn't this monster. That she had to remember.

Nonsense.

Tonight, she would fuck and then taste uncooked landrider, as most Atlantean royal houses did. Mera had to keep the tradition.

Her tongue ran atop her pointy teeth.

Mother would be proud.

CHAPTER 8

MERA GASPED for air as she opened her eyes.

Bast was staring down at her, his lips shaping a relieved smile. "Welcome back, ki—"

She grabbed him by the collar of his shirt, a cold sweat breaking through her body as she nearly slammed her forehead against his. "I'll never be like her! She won't get to me!" she panted. Breathing hurt like on the day she'd stepped out of the ocean for the last time.

"Who are you talking about?" He cupped her shoulders and gently pushed her down, but Mera fought against it. "You're safe." His tone was careful, soft.

Her muscles relaxed slowly, almost as if Bast was singing a spell of his own. Besides, her head hurt, so okay, she laid down again.

Mera glanced around as she rubbed her temple. They were in a big room with old wooden walls, high-ceiling, and floors. Old wood had a way of absorbing scents and liquids over time, which made this place reek of rotting bark and... soup?

Well, it wasn't the worst smell in the world.

A red couch rested on the far end, near a large herbarium with LED lamps shining above tall plants. Plump and red tomatoes hung from the stems, and some peppers, too.

"Where are we?" she asked, her heartbeat steadying.

"Pimpliton. It's a small town in the fae state," he explained. "It's a one day's trip from Tir Na Nog."

Bast's hair was once again up in a loose bun, and thin strands brushed the sides of his face. The image of him, with flowing white hair and black beady eyes flashed in her mind.

Fangs… he had fangs.

No, she must've hallucinated it.

He sat back on a low stool next to her. "So, you had a nightmare?"

"You have no idea."

Mera patted the soft surface beneath her. She was lying on a bed, but whose bed was it?

Lifting the bottom of her shirt, she searched for the spot where the magic dagger had pierced her flesh.

The skin on the area was smooth and flawless. Not a single scar left. Just a red blotch on her shirt, and a slit across the fabric proved that Mera had been wounded.

Bast smiled knowingly. "Like it?" He nodded toward the herbarium. "Stella does impeccable work."

Stella?

A striking female with caramel skin walked away from the plants at that moment. She had the same wide smile as Bast, but where his was savage and untamed, hers was kind and meek. She wore a red dress with golden details that twirled around her from her shoulders to her feet. Like she'd wrapped a fancy sheet around her body, leaving a stripe of her stomach exposed.

Ears that were too pointy to be human, but too round to be fae peeked out from her silky onyx hair, which was tied in a low braid that cascaded down her back. She held a makeshift basket, but Mera couldn't see the contents.

A hint of annoyance prickled in her chest.

Were they together?

Oh, not annoyance, then. Just irrational jealousy.

"Thank you, Stella." Mera mumbled, forcing herself to sit up again. This time, Bast helped. "I take it this is your work?" She pointed to the wound that wasn't there anymore.

"Indeed," Stella said with pride.

"You're one fine healer."

Mera's mind spun and she fell back into Bast's arms.

"You okay, kitten?" He asked, worry oozing from his clear blue eyes as he swiped a strand of russet hair from her cheek. "You're too weak."

They were so close that the tip of their noses nearly touched, their breaths mingling. She opened her mouth to say something, though she couldn't remember what. So she stayed there, stunned, without knowing what to do, when her body made the decision for her. Mera leaned slightly forward.

Following her lead, Bast lowered his head. Their lips drew painstakingly closer…

"Sebastian Dhay!" Stella chided. "The woman is disoriented!" She took a kitchen cloth from the basket, slapping it against the side of his neck. "Don't you dare."

He didn't turn to Stella, his focus entirely on the furious blush that invaded Mera's cheeks. "She's far from disoriented, sis."

"You have a sister?" Mera pushed herself away from him and rubbed her forehead. Poseidon in the trenches, when would her brain stop pounding against her skull?

"Technically, half-sister," Stella corrected as she set the basket atop a kitchen island behind Bast.

Mera had completely missed the kitchen. It blended

perfectly with the rest of the space, being made entirely out of wood, except for the oven. A big pan rested atop the burning fire, and fumes wafted from the contents.

Ah, so that's where the smell of soup came from. Stella scooped a good deal of the liquid into a bowl and brought it to her.

Mera downed it in one go. It tasted savory and sour, and it was hot, but not enough to burn her throat.

Stella's blue eyes, strikingly similar to Bast's, twinkled. "At least *someone* appreciates my cooking." She flicked Bast's shoulder with her finger, then took the empty bowl from Mera's hand, and headed to the kitchen for a refill.

"Hey, I like your cooking," he protested, then seemed to think twice about it. "Most of the time."

"Let's see how long you can put up with him, Mera," Stella added, scooping more soup. "I predict you'll be ready to slap him by the end of the week."

"End of the week? I wanted to do that the moment I met him."

Stella giggled.

Bast gave Mera a sly, sideways grin. "If it were up to me, I'd do better things with you, Detective. Though some slapping might be involved."

Mera's face felt so warm she thought it might melt.

Silver lining, Bast kept being his flirty, snarky, and unbearable self. If he had recognized the macabre, she doubted he would be so relaxed right now. Also, the fact she was still alive, and the lack of police enforcement there proved that he still believed she was human.

Mera let out a deep breath and looked up at the ceiling.

Whoever is up there or in the trenches, thank you.

Stella returned with the bowl and handed it to her. "Eat as much as you can. The kind of healing I do recycles a lot of your own energy. That's why you're weak."

71

"Thanks." She sipped the soup. "How long was I down?"

"Two days," Bast answered casually, and she nearly spit out the soup.

"Two days? Seriously?"

"Healing takes time and energy on both sides," Stella explained. "Two days is normal, especially for a deadly wound. Besides, it took at least half a day for Bast to get you here."

Mera frowned at him. "You did a day's trip in half the time?"

"It was either that or let you die." His shoulders rose and fell casually, as though his statement meant nothing.

"I fixed his wings once you were out of danger." Stella tapped the top of her brother's head with care. "They were such a mess. Clenched tendons, swollen muscles… a complete train wreck. No pun intended."

Mera blinked at him, words failing her. "I can't thank you enough, Bast."

"You're my partner, kitten. We're supposed to take care of each other, right?"

Worry suddenly hit her like a wrecking ball. "Crap! Did you warn the Cap?"

"Of course I did. She wants you to call her." He picked up Mera's phone from a dresser near the bed and handed it to her. The fact she hadn't lost it when all shit went to hell was nothing short of a miracle. "But finish your soup first."

'Yes, sir,' her siren mocked.

Once Mera was done, she dialed in and put the call on speaker.

The Cap picked up on the first ring. She told Mera to be careful and trust no one, not even Bast. And yes, Ruth knew they were on speaker; she simply didn't care.

She also told them that Bast's decision to avoid hospitals had been smart, since whoever was behind the bounty could strike again, and Mera, being *human*, was an easy target.

She then pushed to know where they were, but Bast and Stella shook their heads hurriedly.

"Hmm, we're safe," Mera assured her.

"Fine, don't tell me. Detective Dhay," the Cap said, "I applaud your fast thinking, but if Detective Maurea had died, you and I would be having a very different conversation."

"Yes, Captain." He saluted her mockingly. Mera was glad Ruth couldn't see him, or he'd be a dead fae.

"Cap, the witch mentioned a psychic who apparently saw Bast killing a male. We think the same male might have ordered the hit on him."

Seers were a sham, any reasonable creature knew that.

Old hag Ursula had once foreseen Mera leading an army of Atlanteans into battle, but that was no vision, just a hallucination caused by the rotting algae she ate to *"open a channel to the afterlife."*

Yes, ordering someone's death because of a silly vision seemed extreme, but not impossible.

"People have murdered for less," the Cap admitted from the other side. "It's a solid theory. This could be the same person who killed Zev Ferris and Sara Hyland."

"That's possible," Bast agreed, then winked at Mera. "If we catch them, we solve the case. And then, I'll become your partner permanently."

A void and butterflies both gnawed at her stomach. Mera didn't know how to feel about that.

No more late nights working with Julian and ordering Chinese takeout. No more roaming the streets together and solving cases... Her chest ached, but a part of her looked forward to working with Bast. Which wasn't fair or logical.

"Indeed, Detective Dhay," Ruth went on from the other side. "Your captain told me he has scheduled a visit to the

Summer King's place in two days. Can you meet that deadline?"

"Yes," Bast assured.

"Good. Stay sharp, you two. And, cookie—"

"I'll be careful," Mera promised.

The moment they hung up, Bast let go of the laugh he was holding. "Cookie?" He slapped his leg. "And you were giving me a hard time because I called you kitten!"

"It's different," she snapped. "The Cap raised me. You, on the other hand, I've known for two days."

"Four." He waved his hand dismissively. "You were unconscious, but it counts."

Stella slapped the nape of Bast's neck. "Don't let him fool you, Mera. There's a good fae underneath," she motioned to him from head to toe, "this."

Was there?

Mera remembered the cruel darkness that had taken hold of him, the ravenous monster that ached for violence.

Deciding to change the subject, she set her phone aside. "How was growing up with this douche, Stella?"

Bast and his sister exchanged a glance filled with sadness.

"It wasn't easy, but not because of him." Stella took the bowl from the bed and went to the kitchen.

Mera bit her bottom lip, wondering if she should ask what had been on her mind since meeting Bast's sister. "Does it have anything to do with your ears?"

"She's a halfling." He crossed his arms. "Thanks for pointing out the obvious."

"Bast," Stella scolded him.

He was only being protective. It was kind of cute.

"I thought halflings were insanely powerful," Mera confessed. "It's the real reason why the light courts forbid fae mating with other magical creatures, right?"

Stella nodded from the kitchen, raising her arm. Thick,

black fur grew atop it, and her fingers morphed into sharp claws.

Werewolf.

The shift lasted only a moment, and soon, Stella's arm turned back to normal.

"Halflings *may* be incredibly powerful, but since Bock the Conqueror, in the twelfth century, none of us has actually displayed immense power," Stella explained as she washed the bowl. "The light courts ignore the Agreement of Cordiality more out of prejudice than actual fear." She closed the tap and dried the bowl. "The Night Court allows interracial mating, but cheating on your spouse is frowned upon. Which means bastards like me—"

"No." Bast winced as if he'd tasted something bitter. "Don't call yourself that."

Stella turned to them and rolled her eyes. "—*those* like me are pariahs. Quite literally."

"You don't owe Mera an explanation," he grumbled under his breath.

Stella walked to them, drying her hands on a kitchen cloth. "I want to tell her. I'm not ashamed of who I am, big brother."

Oh, Mera really liked Stella.

She had a ton of questions, but figured she'd prodded enough. Besides, this seemed to be a touchy subject, especially for Bast.

"All right." He stood and clapped his hands. "Let's get going."

"What? No!" Stella cried. "Mera, you're still groggy from the magic I used to heal you. It can stupefy someone for weeks! I'm surprised you woke up so soon."

"I'll take care of her," Bast assured with a wicked grin. "Besides, Mera is a tough *cookie*."

Oh, she wanted to punch him in the face so hard.

Stella glared at Mera, silently asking for back up.

"I would love to stay," and she truly would, "but we have a case to solve, and time is of the essence."

Stella puffed air through her lips. "Fine. But you must take it easy for a while. No matter what this ass says." She elbowed Bast's ribs and he faked an *"ouch!"*

Mera nodded, holding down a chuckle. "I will. Thank you so much for your help, Stella." She pushed herself to her feet way too quickly, nearly toppling over, but Bast caught her.

This seemed to be a habit for him.

Once again, here they were, stupidly close. His strong arm wrapped around her, pressing her against the side of his body, yet Mera pushed away. Bast was a living magnet, but she had to resist his pull.

"What's the plan?" she finally asked once she was certain she could stand on her own two feet without falling. "We lost our luggage and my gun."

"No, we didn't. I went back to fetch everything once Stella got you stable and healed my wings." He nodded to the two duffel bags on the floor, near the feet of the bed.

Only then did Mera notice that Bast's vest and shirt, which should have been riddled with her blood—and his— were completely clean.

She frowned at him. "You went back just because of the luggage?"

Hissing through his teeth, he scratched the nape of his neck. "I *may* have also gotten rid of the witch's body."

Mera gasped. "What?"

"I told your Captain that I injured her, but she escaped." His face crumpled in annoyance. "Oh, come on, kitten. Don't look at me like that."

"Hiding a body is illegal, Bast!"

"So is killing someone."

"But you had to! You saved my life."

Well, as far as he knew. Bast didn't suspect Mera had the witch trapped under the macabre, and if it was up to her, he never would.

"Yes, I killed her to save you, but a kill is a kill. I would be stuck in hearings that would take forever, and the case would go cold." He threw his hands up in the air. "You would love it, of course. You're dying to get back to that partner of yours, but guess what? They would assign you to another fae, and trust me, you were lucky to get me."

She stared at him, heart pounding in her ears. "It's still wrong."

This went against everything the Cap had taught her.

To protect and serve.

Not that the woman hadn't bent the rules occasionally to help Mera, but there was a line.

She understood Bast, though. Hiding the body might not be the prettiest or most honorable decision, but the case came first, and the witch had already delayed them enough.

"Fine." Mera pinched the bridge of her nose, knowing she had just turned into his accomplice. *Concealment of a body.* A good year in jail, at least. "You did what you had to do. But if someone's after you, we'll need to keep a low profile. So, where are we staying?"

Stella opened her mouth, probably to say they should stay there, but Mera wouldn't have it.

"Absolutely not. If someone is after your brother, it means our presence puts you in danger." She turned to Bast, who watched her with... pride? Adoration? She couldn't really decipher him. "Where are we heading?"

A smile hooked on the left side of Stella's cheek. "She's as bad as you are, big brother."

"She tries," he taunted, his focus locked on Mera. "I know the perfect place, kitten."

CHAPTER 9

Mera and Bast spent the entire day on bus and local train rides toward the outskirts of Tir Na Nog, and even though night had already fallen, they still hadn't reached their destination.

The wooden bus they found themselves in was packed with lower fae Mera had only seen in books.

She and Bast had been sitting across from a grumpy troll for nearly an hour. He had lime-green skin and a long, hooked nose, and he busied himself with reading the newspaper. He also reeked of rotten eggs, which, according to Bast, was a big part of their diet.

Not far from them, a goblin with three horns atop his head chatted with a hairy pooka, with the face of a rabbit and the body of a monkey. They both wore black suits and driver's caps, and Mera overheard the words *"baku"* and *"ghalle."*

Bast had explained *"baku"* meant something like asshole or idiot, depending on the intonation. *"Ghalle"* might mean boss—if she remembered her lessons from school correctly.

She couldn't hold back the smile that spread on her lips as

she watched sprites gossiping eagerly in Faeish, and imps, with skin the color of dawn, working on crossword puzzles on the newspaper.

Right then, the fae and human worlds didn't seem so different.

"*Mahit' na ke nua: Pat te, slums.*" The muffled voice from the driver, a Sidhe with azure skin and black hair, resonated through thin air.

Slums?

Could it mean the same as it did in English?

"That's our stop, kitten," Bast whispered from beside her, and a certain dread filled Mera's chest.

The bus soon came to a halt, and Bast and Mera pushed around the passengers to get off it. Once they stepped out, she inhaled deeply, filling her lungs with fresh, crispy night air.

Say what you will about trolls and goblins, but they didn't enjoy showering often, and it showed. Well, it *smelled*.

Two honks came from the bus, and Mera turned to watch the long wooden vehicle jerk back into movement. It drove away on its wooden wheels, entirely fueled by magic.

"Shall we?" Bast asked from behind her.

He led her to a small road that pierced through dense bushes, only to end in a vast square.

Mera's jaw hung when she took in what had to be the slums of Tir Na Nog.

Dirt roads went into several directions up the mountain, edged by colorful makeshift houses that seemed to pile atop one another. Chiming music, different from anything she'd ever heard and yet oddly familiar, rang from everywhere as the scent of cooked meals spread in the air.

Warm lights that resembled billions of fireflies decorated the dirt paths and houses, hanging above lamp posts. This wasn't magic, though. The lights were connected by plastic conduits that were nearly invisible against the dark of the night.

Electricity.

Tir Na Nog might vocally reject technology, but they certainly enjoyed it when necessary.

"Most houses in the slums have electric devices," Bast explained as they followed one of the narrow paths up the mountain. "Lower fae don't have enough magic to conserve food for long, and they can't create fire with a simple thought, either. Most of them, such as ogres and trolls, also don't have wings, which explains the buses."

"You have wings, but we traveled by bus and train," she countered mindlessly, observing the lively, colorful chaos around them.

He lifted his luggage and raised one eyebrow at her. "I'm not a beast of burden."

"What a nice way of saying lazy." Mera assessed their surroundings, feeling a lightness in her chest. "Electricity and public transportation in Tir Na Nog. It feels like a step forward, Bast."

Even if the buses were made of wood and fueled by magic. Maybe one day, faeries would finally accept human technology.

One could dream.

"Glad you like it," he offered as they continued.

They passed by a variety of lower fae who strolled around, while others chilled by the sidewalk with their families, or talked to each other eagerly. A group of banshees on the left sang songs and played guitars, while pooka children danced to the tune.

None of the lower fae cast a second glance at them as they went, which was odd since Bast was a Sidhe and Mera a human—by all accounts.

She did spot a handful of Sidhe as they went, though not

many. Some were Winter fae with white hair and skin, while others belonged to the Night Court, with moon-silver hair and darker complexions.

The majority of the Sidhe she found, however, belonged to the light courts. Not that all fae looked the same, but a female with pink skin and yellow curls likely belonged to Spring. A hurrying male with a red mane and green eyes probably came from Autumn, and a boy with tanned skin and dark hair, yelling for his mother's attention, surely must belong to Summer.

Granted, it was a biased way of seeing things. After all, Stella was a child of Night and had ebony hair.

She nodded to the Sidhe. "I figured most members of the courts lived in the center of the borough."

Bast peered at them with a certain sorrow. "In a place with too many kings, no king stays in power for long."

They passed a couple of humans—probably there illegally —but they also didn't seem surprised to see them.

'Maybe they think you're Bast's whore,' her siren whispered. *'You should play the part.'*

Mera ignored the bastard, continuing to follow the narrow dirt road that led to the upper parts of the mountain.

The chaos from the lower levels slowly waned, leaving Mera and Bast surrounded by a deep quiet as the electric fireflies shone across their path. They finally reached a brick house with a pointy roof that bent to the right. Mera remembered building a gingerbread house once with the Cap, but it'd come out crooked and with an uneven ceiling.

It looked awfully similar to that one.

As soon as Bast touched the wooden door with his palm, the entrance clicked open. He stepped aside to let her in first.

"It's… peculiar." Mera muttered as she entered the place.

The upper corners of the light blue walls were chipping, and she almost tripped over a broken floor tile. She couldn't decide if the flooring was originally white or gray because of how dirty it looked.

The curtains framing the windows were tattered on the edges, like thousands of moths had chewed on them. The style of the open kitchen was a bit old, as in from fifty years ago, but at least the fridge and oven—both with ceramic doors and handles—appeared to be in working order.

Mera wondered if she should check the bathroom and bedroom, but decided not to proceed. For now, at least.

The wooden door creaked loudly when Bast closed it. He dropped his bag on the floor, spreading his arms wide. "Welcome to my palace."

She glanced around. "Peachy."

"I used this place as a hideout when I first arrived in the continent," Bast said as he opened the windows, letting in fresh air. "I come here whenever I can. Especially when I don't want to be found."

Mera wondered why he'd needed a hideout in the first place, but decided not to ask. As she'd learned from Stella, Bast's past could be a tricky subject.

"None of the fae seemed surprised to see a Sidhe with a human," Mera noted instead, as she set her bag atop a brown leather couch that faced a coffee table.

Those were the only pieces of furniture in the living room, aside from a round dining table with two chairs near the kitchen. Unlike the rest of the house, the furniture looked new and well kept, so that was a plus.

"People from the slums don't judge." Bast shrugged. "Either that, or they thought you were my whore."

Her siren smiled eagerly. *'Let's prove them right!'*

Down, girl.

Bast headed to the fridge and grabbed two beers. "I love it here. The place could use some renovation, but it's still pretty great."

Clearly, he was blind. Or at the very least, he saw this place through thick, rose-colored glasses.

He handed her a bottle and clinked it against his own in a toast. "Also, the view is amazing."

He did have a point. The center of Tir Na Nog—which might be the size of Clifftown, maybe bigger—stood magnificent in the distance, half circled by mountains with glittering lights just like the ones from these slums.

The fae constructions differed from human architecture, which was mostly formed of sharp rectangles, with glassy façades that reached out to the sky.

Clean. Efficient. Lifeless.

Fae buildings, on the other hand, resembled palaces from faerie tales, filled with curves, rococo swirls, and smooth, colorful shapes that built atop one another.

Some of the constructions did reach for the sky, like that white building—or was it a castle?—which built atop itself in the way of a fancy wedding cake. Mera narrowed her eyes to spot vines drooping down the balconies, shaping green waterfalls.

Still, skyscrapers such as this were an exception in Tir Na Nog.

One glass building did resemble the ones from back home. It stuck out from the rest of the city like a sore thumb, but it was only a few floors high. Probably where the embassy and border agency were located—ridiculous since it all belonged to Hollowcliff. She guessed Bast's precinct might be in there too, but she would find out sooner or later.

Far in the distance, beyond the valley occupied by the borough, Mera could almost spot the ocean.

She took a long gulp of her beer. It wasn't as bitter as the ones from Clifftown, and it went down her throat smoothly. "This is good."

"It's fae ale." Bast watched the view, his jaw set. "Down we go, into the lion's den."

Biting her lower lip, she nodded to the city ahead. "I must admit that as a human, I'm not looking forward to waltzing down those streets."

"Don't worry, you'll be safe. Most fae who despise humans are big players who don't mingle with the rest of us. You might face some resistance from snobby Sidhe, but that's all." His attention never left Tir Na Nog. "They say this city chews you up and spits out the bones. But the truth is, Tir Na Nog is what we make of it. For that, it's merciless and perfect." He nudged her shoulder with his arm. "And you're a tough *cookie*."

She chuckled. "Ass."

A moment of silence passed between them.

"Hey, did the witch call you a prince, or did I get that wrong?"

"I used to be a prince, yes," he admitted quietly. "I ran away from that a long time ago, kitten. Not that it made a difference. There are hundreds of princes throughout the fae state, didn't you know? Light and dark, and these are just the Seelie Courts. If you count the Unseelie…" He blew a whistle. "Too many princes to count."

"But how many Night princes are there?"

"Five." He nodded slowly to the view. "Do you know why I joined the police?"

She shook her head, seeing through his diversion but knowing better than to push.

"The fae state, kingdom back then, rejected nightlings and icelings after the civil war. Until the unification, Night and Winter fae couldn't set foot in the kingdom. Once it all became Tagrad, the government fought for our rights, going head-to-head with the light courts until they struck a deal."

He turned to her with a certain melancholy behind his

eyes. "How could I not fight for the country that brought me back home?"

"Detective Dhay, you have more layers than I assumed." She clinked her bottle with his, and took another gulp of her beer. "Does every night fae have magic like yours?"

A merciless force that destroyed everything in its path.

"Not really. Magic is wild and feral, but once tamed, it adapts to its owner." Finishing his beer, he placed the empty bottle on the coffee table. "It's why no magic is ever the same."

If Bast truly had his magic under control, which she highly doubted when she remembered those ravenous beady eyes, why had it been so... destructive?

"You had fangs," she blurted.

He cocked his head left, considering her words. "I also have wings, but you don't see them all the time."

"Hiding who you are from others seems to be a habit for you," she noted.

Funny how much they had in common.

"Life in Tir Na Nog is an ongoing battle," he scoffed. "Hiding what I can do from others is not only an advantage, but it often means my survival. So yes, I watch my own skin."

She raised her beer bottle to him. "Nothing wrong with that."

He gave her a sad grin. "The problem, kitten, is that the main courts—Summer, Autumn, Spring—hold too much power in this state." The impact of the sentence hung in the air between them. "Many fae in my precinct are like me. Pariahs, who don't belong with the mighty *light*. And still, you can't trust them because the light courts influence every-thing and everyone."

"Find an honest faerie and you find gold," Mera muttered the saying she'd overheard countless times in her precinct.

"Indeed." Bast's forehead crumpled as he watched the city.

"My Captain is the most honest fae I know, but he must cede to the courts' power every now and then. I doubt any other captain in all the boroughs goes through the same."

She nearly choked on her beer. "There are fae foolish enough to tell your captain what to do?"

Heck, Mera had never seen someone do that to Ruth. Even her superiors walked on a very thin line when dealing with her.

The woman scared them shitless.

Bast chuckled without any humor. "You know why he's Captain? The king of the Autumn Court exiled him, because he denounced a duke who had a human slave to the authorities. Before the unification, this would've cost him his head, but Hollowcliff police picked him up and enlisted him."

"That's horrible," she mumbled, a grim sensation prickling in her chest.

"It's Tir Na Nog, kitten."

"How are the courts allowed to exile someone who was abiding to Tagradian law? That's… insane."

"The light courts don't recognize most of our laws, and when they do, it's because of police reinforcement." He shrugged. "They've been getting more daring recently, Danu knows why."

Her fingertip tapped the neck of her bottle in thought. "In that context, the Summer King's murder seems… convenient."

"I can't say I'm sorry to see him go," he admitted. "But I'm a detective first, and a bastard with a grudge second."

Her elbow softly knocked against his side. "Smartass."

Bast undid his bun and set it higher. "I do love my job, you know. Bringing justice to those who have no voice. Going against the light courts as much as I can, without fucking over my precinct and Captain. It's the first thing that has fulfilled me since..." He turned to the window and frowned. "I can't remember."

They watched the landscape in silence for a while, until Mera finished her beer and set it on the coffee table.

"So, what should I expect tomorrow?" she asked. "What's the Summer Court like? Considering everything you told me, I can't interrogate them the same way as I do everyone else."

Observing her the way a feline watches a mouse, he approached slowly. Poseidon in the trenches, how she hated getting so easily lost in those blue eyes, ensnared by his strong, woodsy scent. And his body, damn it, it spoke to her, like the songs her kind used to sing to lure sailors.

"We have to walk on eggshells to get their cooperation," he admitted, his tone low and hoarse as he halted too close to her. Damn fae had some serious boundary issues. "We have to feign respect and humility. Be submissive." Slowly licking his lips, he leaned closer. "Are you ready for that?" he whispered softly at the curve of her neck.

Her hands fisted as every inch of her body tensed in response to him. "I can do submissive."

"Hm, I would love to see that," he spoke lowly, the corner of his mouth brushing her cheek.

With the last inch of courage she had, Mera stepped away and crossed her arms. "You had too much beer."

"Sure, let's blame it on the alcohol." He winked at her, then went to his bag. Pulling out a black shirt, he set it atop the kitchen counter. "Also, don't eat or drink anything they offer."

Bast began unbuttoning his vest and nodded to a door close to the kitchen. "You can sleep in my bedroom."

Mera barely recorded what he'd said. She couldn't take her eyes off him.

He threw the vest on the sofa and proceeded to unbutton

his shirt, a burning dare in his eyes. Mera took in his strong, defined abs, and a delirious warmth went down her spine.

He tossed the shirt atop the sofa too, showcasing his perfect chiseled torso and strong biceps, meant to wrap around a woman as she rode his...

"Enjoying the show, are we?" He began undoing his belt, his deceiving, sharp eyes burning with lust.

Mera's throat was so dry it might be made of sand. "I..."

Noticing the massive bulge underneath his black boxer briefs, she stepped forward. She wanted, needed, to touch that part of him; lick it, hold it, shove it inside her until...

No!

This was wrong. He was her partner, at least for the time being.

"Stop being a dick, Detective Dhay." Grasping her bag, she hurried into the bedroom, slamming the door closed behind her. Her rushed breaths rang loudly in her ears.

'Idiot,' her siren grumbled.

CHAPTER 10

ACCORDING TO BAST, the Summer King's three-story penthouse occupied the last floors of the wedding cake building she'd spotted yesterday, one of the tallest constructions in town. He'd also told her that a third of the entire Summer Court—the second most powerful after Autumn—lived inside the structure.

The building's vast entrance hall resembled a giant cave entirely made of gold. Three elevators were located at the back, and a round, white-marbled helpdesk stood at the center of the space. Summer fae strolled about, paying them no attention.

Bast led Mera to the main desk, his steps clanking against the shining floor. He showed his badge to the guard, a bark-skinned fae with golden hair and uniform, who seemed to blend in with his surroundings.

"We have an appointment," he said.

The fae eyed Bast and Mera with disgust. "Police only goes in with a warrant."

He spoke in English, which seemed awfully kind of him. And strange, since he clearly didn't like the police.

"Ah, is that so?" Bast eyed his own nails as if he didn't have a worry in the world. "I have to present a warrant to attend a *scheduled* meeting that your queen is well aware of. Am I correct?"

The guard crossed his bulky arms and nodded.

"I don't like to waste my time, Lionel. It's very precious to me," Bast warned casually, but there was a sharp, veiled threat in his tone.

The guard swallowed. "Bimi is in jail because of you, *Detective.*"

"Bimi was selling fae crystal three blocks away from my precinct. Of course I put him in jail. Your bosses hired a Sidhe in our team to get rid of the evidence, as they often do, but guess what, asshole?" He leaned forward on the counter and bared his teeth. "That corrupt fucker is in jail, too."

"Fuck you, Sebastian."

"Always a charmer." He knocked on the desk's marbled surface. "Will we do this the easy or the hard way? I'm up for both."

Lionel, who was taller and a lot bulkier than her partner, gulped. He glanced at Bast, then at Mera. "Fine, but the human stays."

"The human goes," Mera added pointedly. "And if you were speaking in English just to intimidate me, it didn't work."

Bast raised his shoulders. "My partner bites, Lionel." Swiveling on his feet, he went to the elevators, leaving a flabbergasted guard behind.

Mera followed him.

"I thought they'd give me a hard time for being human," she said as the elevator's glassed doors opened, and they got into it.

"Light courts hate the police as much as they hate humans." Bast pressed the top button on the panel, then shoved his hands in his pockets as the elevator began to ascend.

The anxious tapping of Mera's foot on the glass floor echoed around them, while her eyes wandered toward her left, taking in the full view of Tir Na Nog. Shifting right, she noticed the building's stories rush by them through the glass doors, but she couldn't hear the grinding of engines or motors in the background. "Let me guess, the elevator's fueled by magic."

"Of course," he said. "We could've flown to the penthouse's balcony—most fae use them as landing pads. But I figured we shouldn't barge in like that."

She nodded. "We have to play nice."

Winking at her, Bast laid his head back on the glass wall. "We can try."

The elevator soon opened to a big main foyer.

One of the help—a sprite with green skin and hair, who wore a golden maid's uniform and a white apron—greeted them before going to fetch Lisandra Ferris, Zev Ferris' wife, and queen of the Summer Court.

Well, at least the sprite had been more courteous than Lionel.

White marble covered the floors and stretched wall to wall, deep into the arch that separated the entrance from an enormous living room. A golden chandelier carrying hundreds of unlit candles floated near the ceiling—an enchanted object, like the wooden buses that cut across town, and the building's fancy elevators.

White roses twirled around the golden rails of the marbled staircase on their right, which led to the second and third floors. The golden baseboards lining the bottom of the marbled walls had to cost more than Mera's yearly salary. And the golden entrance hall at the ground floor… fuck, that must be enough to buy a small island.

"Are all royals this excessive?" she whispered to Bast.

He waved his hand dismissively. "This is nothing, kitten."

The sprite returned, bowing slightly at them. "The queen will see you in the living room."

The first thing Mera noted when they entered the space, were the five rococo archways that led into an enormous balcony outside, allowing daylight to flood the entire penthouse. Golden curtains hung beside the archways, fluttering against soft breezes.

She then studied the parade of invaluable paintings which hung on the left wall, facing a beige sofa in the middle of the room. An exact copy of the chandelier from the entrance hung midair, above the sofa, and a round carpet made of white peacock feathers stretched underneath the seating.

"*Esses thu*, Sebastian Dhay?" A high-pitched voice rang from the right.

Under an arched passage that led to another room in the penthouse, stood a female with straight red hair that fell like a waterfall past her pointy ears. Gold, hoop earrings decorated her lobes in the same fashion as her dead husband.

The faerie wore a sleeveless green dress that highlighted her straight chest and collarbone, the sleek fabric hugging all the curves she didn't have. A golden headband encrusted with green emeralds pulled her hair back.

Oh wait. It wasn't a headband.

It was a crown.

Mera was familiar with those.

"Hello, Lisandra," Bast greeted as a muscle ticked in his jaw, his body tense with fake cordiality. "My colleague doesn't speak Faeish, so could we stick to the first national language?"

First National language. A polite jab at their host.

Lisandra stepped down into the living room, her attention never leaving him. "I'd heard you'd gone the public route. Who could've imagined." Craning her neck left, she clicked her tongue. "Pity, really. You were the best shag I've ever had, but now, only this revolting whore you brought to my property would take you."

'Anytime, bitch,' her siren growled.

Mera wanted to slap that stuck-up faerie senseless, but she had a job to do, and she had to be meek.

Submissive.

With a smirk, Bast took Lisandra's hand, kissing it, then licked her skin with the tip of his tongue. Slowly. Gently. The way one would when...

Lisandra drew a shaggy breath.

"Charming as always, your majesty," Bast offered, his tone low and rough. The bastard knew the effect he had on women.

He knew it very well.

Fire spread inside Mera's chest. Sure, he'd done that to humiliate Lisandra in his own way, but did he need to kiss her hand in an over-sexualized way? Really?

Her siren let out a longing sigh. *'I wonder what that tongue of his can do...'*

Shut up!

"Queen Lisandra," Mera started, trying to ignore the urge to punch the damn fae. "Thank you for having us. We'd like to ask you a few questions about your husband, Zev Ferris."

The faerie shot her a wolfish grin. She snapped her fingers and the same sprite who had welcomed them stepped into the living room.

"May I offer you something to drink, Detective?" she asked. "The greatest delicacies in the world are available at your request."

Nice try.

"No, thanks. I'm fine."

Lisandra's red lips became a thin line as she waved the maid away. "You've taught your human pet well, Sebastian."

He rubbed the bridge of his nose. "What was the plan, Lisandra? Turn her into a toad?"

"Of course not. You know I'm much more sophisticated than that." She eyed Mera up and down. "I'd turn your pet into a bug and squash her with my foot."

"That's enough," Bast snapped, then closed his eyes as if chiding himself. "Captain Asherath told me I would have your full collaboration. Was he wrong?"

"No." Lisandra shrugged. "Do remember, however, that you're here because *I* want my husband's killer found. If my independent contractors weren't so worthless, I'd never have allowed Tagradian police inside my home."

"If you need us, you better play nice," Mera warned.

Lisandra's lips parted as if she couldn't believe Mera had dared to threaten her. Before queen bitch could complain, Mera pulled out her notepad and pen from her jacket's inside pocket.

"Were you aware that your husband had a drug problem?" she asked. "We found considerate amounts of fae crystal in his blood—"

"Out!" Lisandra yelled, not at Mera, but at the two brownies who'd entered the space to dust the furniture. "Now!"

They scurried away, dropping their dusters in a trembling hurry.

The Summer Queen took a recomposing breath. "I was aware. My husband had a court of fifty thousand on his shoulders. We provide jobs, sustenance, and trade to our people. Being the center of our family, of our court… It took its toll."

"Do the circumstances of your husband's death seem odd to you?"

"Of course!" Lisandra raised her chin. "He was murdered by his human drug dealer. The despicable worm probably drugged him senseless before doing the deed."

Bast shook his index finger. "You're telling this to your court, but the police informed you about the details of his passing. Specifically, that Sara Hyland was already dead by the time your husband found her. Also, remember that you're legally bound to tell us the truth."

"I'm bound to nothing. Your laws are not my laws, *Tagradian*," she snapped, as if Bast was a dirty traitor.

He raised his brow. "Funny. Your ID says the same, Tagradian *kuata*."

That one was easy. "Kuata" meant "sister".

"A ridiculous piece of paper means nothing to me." Huffing, she nodded at Mera. "Next question, *pesut*." Her lips curled with the word, as if pesut meant piece-of-trash.

Fine, then.

"Were you aware your husband was seeing his drug dealer? Romantically, I mean."

Fury burned inside the queen's green irises. "I will not be humiliated in my own home."

"We're not humiliating you." Mera held the urge to roll her eyes. "We're trying to solve your husband's murder. And if you keep dragging out the investigation, we'll start thinking you might've been involved in his death."

Lisandra stepped closer, nearly slamming her flat chest against Mera's own. Only now did she realize the Summer Queen was as tall as Bast, but if things came to it, Mera could easily kick that living twig's ass.

"Dirty whore. You better understand to whom you speak," Lisandra snapped through gritted teeth. Magic thrashed in the queen's core before a red miasma whipped atop her skin.

It smelled like strawberries and rust.

Bast took out his pad and pen from his vest's pocket and began scribbling. "Lisandra, I'd hate to write you down for a misdemeanor. Can you imagine the scandal if I took you down to the station in cuffs?"

Being submissive was clearly hard for Bast, but he was much better at it than Mera. To her own credit, though, she hadn't yet punched the Summer Queen, so she called that a win.

Lisandra chortled. "You wouldn't dare, Sebastian."

A raging darkness swirled in the serenity of his blue eyes, a gaze sharper than daggers that sent shivers down Mera's spine. "Try me."

Lisandra swallowed dry. She must know what Bast was capable of, and it clearly frightened her.

Shooting him a fake grin, she gave in. "I'll collaborate, *inspector*."

"Good. Let's say you were disgruntled given your recent loss, and that you apologized to Detective Maurea, yes?"

She eyed him with raw fury. "Get done with your business and leave."

"Did your husband have any enemies?" When Lisandra glared at Bast as if he was daft, he corrected himself. "Did he have enemies who hated him enough to kill the woman he might have loved?"

"You're casting a wide net, Detective." Someone answered from behind them.

Mera turned to see a male dressed nearly identically to Zev Ferris. He had an open linen shirt that showcased ridiculously ripped abs, black leather pants, and an array of golden looped earrings lining the edges of his pointy ears. A trimmed goatee and strong eyebrows decorated his sun-kissed skin. His reddish, shoulder length hair was straight and slightly mussed.

'Hmm, after-sex hair,' her siren purred. *'This one knows how to have fun. Maybe we could join in next time.'*

You unbearable horny bastard!

The faerie approached with a charming grin and shook Mera's hand, which was a near miracle considering how stuck-up these Sidhe could be. "I'm Zachary Ferris. Son of the late king."

"The heir," Bast added as Zachary also shook his hand.

"Yes, and probably the main suspect since I'd benefit the most from my father's death. But I assure you, detectives, I did nothing to him or that poor woman."

At least Zachary wasn't in denial like Lisandra, and he seemed eager to help.

The Summer Prince went to the middle of the living room, facing them... well, he focused on Mera, not Bast. "Forgive my mother's behavior. She's stuck in the old ways. I, however, see a collaboration between our kinds as essential to keeping Hollowcliff, and all of Tagrad, united."

If Mera hadn't been on duty, she would've swooned over such a charming prince. Then again, she swooned over Bast constantly, even when she was working.

So... yeah.

'You're lucky there's a sofa between you and the prince,' her siren cooed. *'Otherwise...'*

Otherwise nothing, you ass.

"Prince Ferris." Bast cleared his throat. "The woman found with your father carried a fetus with magical DNA, but the child wasn't his."

The cap had phoned in with the puzzling results that morning. It only added to the mystery of the case.

"We believe the woman was used as bait," Bast continued. "Were you aware of their relationship?"

"Unfortunately, no." He rested both hands on his waist. "Father occasionally enjoyed the pleasures of human flesh, but it was always with different women." He eyed Mera with a hint of lust, and Bast's nostrils flared.

"How about you?" He asked drily. "Do you enjoy human flesh, Prince Ferris?"

"Sometimes. Humans can be extremely titillating. Don't you agree, Detective?" Eyeing Mera up and down, he licked his lips. "Fine specimens, they are."

Poseidon in the trenches, she blushed. Mera couldn't believe she'd given this faerie the satisfaction. He was clearly teasing her, but her thirsty siren loooved the attention.

"Where were you on the night of September the second?" Bast pushed, his face a stone mask.

"At a party downtown. Not that our city is riddled with those cameras humans love so much." He shrugged apologetically to Mera. "I hope the testimony from my friends will suffice. I'll ask them to collaborate, of course. I want to help in any way I can."

"We appreciate it. Thank you." Mera narrowed her eyes at Lisandra, who stepped closer to her son. "Where were you on the day of the murders?"

Ignoring her, the queen turned to Bast. "Tell your pet I was enjoying the company of a friend."

"Which friend?" Bast asked as he scribbled on his notebook.

Lisandra seemed taken aback by that, but answered nonetheless. "Barrow Sundgin."

"King of the Autumn Court, and your cousin, if I recall correctly. Interesting." Bast nudged Mera with his elbow as he wrote on his pad. "By *company*, she means they were fucking."

"Excuse me!" Lisandra snapped. "My husband wasn't faithful, so why should I be? He fucked everything with two legs without regard for my honor, for our family, for anything. Only his damn cock mattered!" She spewed the words as if vomiting.

Mera watched in horror, but from the corner of her eye, she noticed Bast shooting his darkness toward the floor. Neither Zachary nor Lisandra noticed because Mera and Bast were standing behind the couch.

"That unborn bastard was probably his; run your tests again and you'll see!" she went on, tears brimming in her eyes. "That scumbag fucked everyone except his own wife! I'm glad he's dead!"

"Please pardon my mother," Zachary wrapped both arms around her and kissed the top of her head. "As you can imagine, this whole ordeal has been quite difficult for us."

"Absolutely," Bast assured. "We'll be out of your way."

Mera frowned. "We will?"

Widening his eyes at her, his lips curled over his teeth. "Yes, Detective Maurea. Queen Lisandra is clearly under distress."

"Oh, yes. Of course, Detective Dhay," she agreed, catching his cue. She turned to Zachary and Lisandra. "Thank you for your time."

"Thank *you*, detectives, for trying to find my father's killer." Zachary led his mother out of the living room. "Come on, let's get you some rest."

A sprite with red hair and skin, who wore a golden maid's uniform, showed Bast and Mera the way out, and once again, they took the elevator.

"Bast, what—"

He shushed her. "Fae might not favor cameras, but we do have word-triggered spells."

As soon as they left the building and waltzed into the sandstone pebbled street, or maybe it was a sidewalk—she couldn't tell, they all looked the same in a sort of medieval manner—Mera pushed again. "Okay, what did you find?"

"First, Zachary Ferris is a fucking liar."

"Really? I thought he was quite collaborative."

He rolled his eyes. "Of course you did, horny pants."

She slapped his arm, but he didn't seem to mind.

"Come on, kitten! You believed that bullshit about being stronger united? It's been the government slogan for centuries!"

He did have a point. And Zachary's eagerness to please hadn't exactly felt natural.

She crossed her arms and huffed. "Maybe you just don't like him."

"Obviously." He pulled out a phone from his pants' pocket and wiggled it at her.

"You have a mobile phone?"

"Of course not. It caught my attention when sunlight hit the half that wasn't covered under the couch. The maid must have missed it during the cleaning, so I had to distract Lisandra before she saw it, too."

"Wait. You caused her meltdown on purpose?"

He gave her a sideways grin. "Pushing someone's buttons is a specialty of mine." Handing her the phone, he motioned to the screen. "Go on. Work your human magic."

Thankfully, the device wasn't password protected.

The battery was nearly empty, but as Mera scrolled through the screen, hope bloomed in her chest.

"Bast, there's an email account linked to this phone. It's in Zev Ferris' name." Excitement sent her heart beating in a frenzy. "This belonged to him."

They'd hit the freaking lottery!

Mobiles were a must in the human, vamp, and shifter's boroughs, but most fae and witches hated them. Maybe it wasn't the iron they feared. Maybe it was the fact that any technology more advanced than basic electricity was a sort of magic of its own.

A magic they didn't understand.

A magic that threatened theirs.

"Are we really doing this?" she asked, mostly to herself.

It was not just wrong, but illegal. They had practically stolen someone else's property.

First, Bast should have obtained consent from the Summer King's family to take the phone, since it was in their property and not in a crime scene.

Second, he should've bagged the phone with gloves instead of setting his fingerprints all over the device. And third, they should've handed the phone to Bast's precinct instead of checking what was inside themselves, but could they trust them?

Bast had said it himself, the light courts' influence reached *everywhere*.

He furrowed his brow at her, as if she'd said something stupid. "Of course we're doing this."

Well, when in Tir Na Nog...

"First things first." She tapped the screen and blocked the GPS, proceeding to check Zev Ferris' messages.

There were several between him and Sara Hyland. Some were flirtatious but they didn't indicate a romantic relationship. Sara had given him free doses of fae crystal and normal meth in exchange for certain favors. Like when Zev sent his Summer thugs to protect her, during negotiations with a dangerous leopard shifter.

As far as Mera could see, the Summer King was using this phone to communicate solely with Sara. However, Sara's roommate had never seen her with a mobile. They hadn't found one at the crime scene or at the dorm either, which probably meant the killer had taken the phone.

Mera scrolled through the messages until their most recent exchange.

"We need to run away," Sara texted.

"I can't. I'm the Summer King," Zev countered. *"Come to me. I'll keep you safe."*

Two days later, he received one last message from her, just four hours before Sara drew her last breath.

Her message read, *"He knows."*

CHAPTER 11

A MOBILE PHONE was harmless to faeries, but it still scared them. Metal, technology, most of it was taboo in the fae state, which was why Mera had to hide the phone on their way to Bast's house. As soon as they arrived, she dropped on the leather couch and pulled it from the inside pocket of her jacket.

"Once we're done, we can hand in the phone to my captain," Bast said. "He'll do the right thing."

Mera raised one eyebrow at him. "He might put us under investigation."

"He won't."

"Well, I don't trust—"

"I do."

She studied him, trying to decide her next move.

Bast had proved himself an excellent detective. Sure, he might be a bit of a loose cannon, but that was normal for a fae. Also, he'd saved Mera's life, so maybe she should give the guy some credit.

"Fine. But I'll send the phone's contents to my precinct too so they can have a look."

Bast's mouth opened to oppose, when she cut him off. "No offense, but you said it yourself. The light courts have little birds inside your precinct. Even if you trust your cap, he can't work alone. Someone's bound to get involved, and that someone might be trouble."

Bast scoffed as he loosened the collar of his shirt. "We did fine on our own for years, kitten."

"You weren't alone because you had him, and he had you." She tapped the phone to her temple. "Or am I wrong?"

He sighed and crossed his arms, studying his own feet, but he didn't deny it.

"It's just a safety measure," she reassured.

Politics and power plays were a sort of magic in their own; a magic neither Mera nor Bast mastered.

"Fine," he spoke quietly as he headed to the window, watching the landscape ahead.

It was obvious he hated the current state of Hollowcliff P.D. in Tir Na Nog. Sure, most of his peers were corrupt, and Bast himself had to bend the rules to get things done every once in a while—like they did now with the phone. But none of that meant he was a bad cop. At least not in Mera's book.

Turning her attention to the phone, she kept scrolling. "I can't find anything relevant, other than the fact Zev Ferris was really into drugs."

Sara wasn't his only dealer. He had contacts with low fae from the slums, and some vamp criminals.

She checked his gallery and found a ton of pictures. Odd, since fae abhorred photos—some still believed it trapped their souls. They preferred magical paintings, which in retrospect, weren't that different.

A breath caught in her chest. "Bast, Zev was into BDSM. Look, that's the sprite who welcomed us to the penthouse." She showed him the picture of the green female with her back slammed against a wall. She wore a spiked black leather collar, and leather strips around her wrists and ankles. She was fully naked, while her tied hands covered her crotch… but not exactly. Two fingers stuck out and seemed to rub on her sex.

She was pleasing herself.

Bast curled his lips in disgust. "He used his power to take advantage of her."

Mera narrowed her eyes, trying to see what he did. "She seems to be enjoying it." She scrolled to the next pictures, which showed Zev and the sprite in some elaborate positions.

"No, she isn't," Bast snarled. "She's there because she has to be. Maybe he threatened to fire her; maybe he threatened her with something much worse. Hard to tell when it comes to those light court bastards."

"That's a logical assumption, but a little far-fetched, don't you think?" She showed him another picture. "I mean, she's clearly smiling."

Bast gave her his back and waved his hand as if to dismiss her.

Ass.

Mera got up and went to her luggage. She grabbed her laptop and the universal cable charger for her phone, which worked as a USB stick, and returned to the sofa.

Removing his hairband, he let his long silver mane cascade behind him.

Bast took off his vest, then his shirt, but he didn't glance at Mera, a certain anger in the way he moved.

It was painful how well those pants fit around his naked waist.

Was he taking them off too?

"I'm taking a bath," he announced curtly before heading to the bathroom.

Mera watched him go, the hard muscles on his back

moving in perfect synchrony, his tanned skin so smooth it might be made of silk.

Without meaning to, she licked her lips.

'Angry Bast needs to relax,' her siren whispered. *'We can help him.'*

Quiet...

'Sex in the shower,' she pushed. *'Get your ass up right now!'*

Trying to ignore the sound of rushing water that came from the closed door, Mera took a deep breath. She downloaded the contents of the phone, drafted an email to Julian and attached the files. She was about to hit send, but hesitated.

He hadn't called her after the accident.

Mera had been stabbed in the gut by magic and nearly died, but Julian didn't send her an email or a message.

Had he been worried? Did he care?

Shake it off, Maurea, she told herself. *You've got a job to do.*

She hit send and picked up her phone for a video call, hating the fact her heart went a thousand miles per hour.

Julian picked up almost immediately. His hazel eyes were wide, his brow wrinkled with concern, but his features relaxed when he saw her. "Hey, partner."

Partner.

Hearing him say it hurt. Mera was betraying him, not because she would likely become Bast's partner, but because she hadn't told him yet.

He was her best friend. She owed him the truth.

'He didn't call us,' her siren reminded.

Shut up, you petty asshole.

"Hey Jules," she greeted, noticing the precinct behind him. She spotted Phil eating a donut on the far, left corner of the screen. "Listen up. I sent you an email, and—"

"Just got it." He looked away from the phone and scrolled through his computer. "Shit, Mera. If Bast's precinct finds out you copied the phone's contents and sent them to me, we're in trouble. Does he know what you're doing?"

"Yes, and he agrees."

"Does he? What if he blabs to his Captain?"

He could, of course. "I don't know, Jules. I trust him. He saved my life."

Mera spotted something behind his hazel eyes; something close to fear. "You trust the *pixie* all of a sudden? What changed in such a short time?"

"Maybe the fact he saved my freaking life?" she repeated, not bothering to hide the frustration in her tone.

He scratched the back of his neck. "I heard about the attack. Look, as far as we know, that witch was after *him*. Probably still is."

No, she was dead, but Mera couldn't tell him without getting Bast into serious trouble.

"You were collateral, Mer," he went on, "which means Bast is putting you in danger."

"I hardly think—"

"Ask the Cap to reassign you." He ran a hand through his lemon-colored hair, giving himself a disgruntled and inappropriately sexy look. "Come back to the precinct. To the way we were. Don't get involved with the fae. It's not safe."

Something thrashed inside her; something angry and ugly. "If you care so much about me, why didn't you call?"

Great, Mera. Just... great.

He blinked, as if he didn't understand the question.

"I nearly died, Jules." Tears pooled in her eyes. "And you didn't give a fuck."

Staring at her, his lips shaped an 'O'. "Are you serious? The Cap told me what happened *yesterday*. I wanted to call you, but she said I should wait until you called us. Apparently, using a phone in public is a huge problem there?"

Now she felt like an idiot.

Mera rubbed her forehead. "Sorry, Jules. I know you care. It's been a rough couple of days, that's all."

"Yeah, I can see." He leaned closer to the screen. "Mer, you have to come back. I don't like this. I don't like this distance," he whispered.

A blazing sensation flushed her cheeks. "Me neither," she countered quietly. "But I can't go back yet."

Taking a deep breath, he stared at his keyboard. "Okay, I'll run through the files and see if I find something."

"I've sent you my notes, too."

"Ok. Thanks."

Oh, he was pissed. Still, Julian couldn't help but laugh when he read something on his screen. "*'Lisandra Ferris: racist queen bitch'.* I love your descriptions, Mer."

What else did he love about her?

"So, all good?" she asked.

"Yeah, I'll continue the investigation here while you handle the pixies." He pressed his lips in a line. "Be careful, okay? I mean, some houses there enchant humans and use them as slaves. Fairies don't care about Tagradian laws."

She rolled her eyes. "Come on, Jules. Some of them do."

"You mean Bast?" He frowned at her as if she'd suddenly turned into a different person. "Mer, the Tir Na Nog precinct is a charade. It's supposed to convince the rest of us that the fae want to belong, but it's bullshit. Fairies do whatever they want *everywhere* in Tagrad, and no one holds them accountable."

"That's not true," she countered. "Bast and his Captain have a hard time juggling the courts and the government's interests. It's not easy or simple."

"Is that what he told you?"

"No, Jules. I've seen it." Fire went up her head. "Besides, as I've said, I fucking trust him."

How many times would she have to repeat it?

"You shouldn't," he countered. "They're all corrupt."

Truth be told, he wasn't wrong. Not long ago, Mera had believed the same. Still did, actually. But Bast was different. His problem, whatever it was, seemed a lot more complex than simple corruption.

"That's a generalist way of viewing it," she argued. "It's not that simple. Not every faerie is corrupt."

"Bullshit. All fae are nasty, and that partner of yours is no exception."

Sure, most fairies *were* nasty. There were tales of fae enchanting humans, or shifters, into dancing until their feet bled. Others glamoured humans and even vamps—a fae's glamour was stronger than theirs—into eating poop while thinking it was a delicacy. Also, Lisandra herself had said point blank she'd meant to turn Mera into a cockroach and smash her with her shoe.

Yes. Faeries could be sneaky bastards, but Bast was a different kind of bastard. One she could tolerate.

'Oh, we could do much more than just tolerate him...'

"Roger, partner," she said before hanging up on him.

Mera shouldn't be mad at Julian. He was just watching out for her, and deep down, he was right. She'd only known Bast for less than a week. Sure, her gut might tell her he could be trusted, but her brain should have known better.

Mera shut down the laptop and set it aside. Pulling wet wipes from her suitcase—a girl's best friend on any trip—she wiped their fingerprints from the phone. She put the device inside a zip bag and closed it, then set it atop the coffee table.

The bathroom door opened and Bast walked out with a towel wrapped around his waist. Water beads peppered his smooth, tanned skin, dripping down his carved stomach. His clumpy hair stuck to his skin, swirling down his shoulders and chest. And his happy trail... her gaze followed it and the siren hoped, prayed, that the towel would drop.

Mera didn't know much about fae deities, but Bast's Duan must've taken extra time to make him.

He frowned at Mera as if she had a watermelon on her face. "You okay, kitten?"

'Fuck him,' her siren whispered. *'Straddle him and make him see stars, or I swear to Poseidon—'*

She blinked, clearing her throat. "I'm fine."

He crossed his arms, highlighting strong, wet, biceps, and raised one tantalizing eyebrow at her. "Are you certain?"

Thirsty. She was suddenly very thirsty.

"Yes, absolutely." She looked away. If she kept staring at him, her siren would go crazy.

A grim sensation settled in her chest as Mera wondered if her desire for Bast might be clouding her judgement.

"They're all corrupt," Julian's voice echoed in her mind.

She grabbed the plastic bag with the phone and displayed it to him, like she was a five-year-old proudly showing daddy a school project. Her brain had clearly melted into a blob.

"All bagged for tomorrow," she told him.

'That's it!' her siren threw her hands up in the air. *'I'm done playing nice!'*

CHAPTER 12

THE WAVES STROLLED LAZILY past Mera's waist. The fins on her temples shook with anticipation, and she licked her teeth. In the night sky above, the moon shone fiercely.

Mera took in the massive landrider standing before her.

He towered over her with a strong, lean body, his form breaking through moonlight. The male had pointy ears that reminded Mera of her fins, and his blue eyes shone like beacons in the darkness.

She caressed his long, light-silver hair, curling his locks between her fingers. They were so soft...

"Finally," she whispered to herself, her mind feeling light, before panic took over. Drawing a sharp breath, she slammed both hands on her fins to hide them. "Can you see me?"

"Obviously." Grabbing her hands, he set them down slowly. "Why are you covering your ears?"

Mera let out a relieved breath. She might be waterbreaker, but what the landrider saw was the human version of herself.

This wasn't any landrider, though.

Mera knew him.

Bast.

It didn't matter if he thought she was waterbreaker or not. This wasn't the real version of him. Mera was dreaming, she was certain. The Bast standing here was a product of her imagination, nothing more.

She studied him through narrowed eyes, noticing each perfect shape. Dream-Bast looked exactly like the real thing. Even his musky scent mingled with the salty tang of the ocean.

Mera bit her bottom lip. Her subconscious had done an outstanding job.

He's mine.

He watched her curiously, his burning gaze sliding down to her breasts. "Sebastian Dhay, what a marvelous dream you're having."

So, Dream-Bast thought he was dreaming? That was really meta.

He unglued his attention from her naked body with a certain effort, and glanced at the night sky, then at the ocean. "I've never been here before. Have I?"

"It's Clifftown shore," she explained.

'Wake up...' her own voice whispered from far away, but the order vanished from her mind as fast as it had come.

Mera blinked. "What are you doing here?"

Taking her hand, he pressed its back against his lips. "I could ask you the same. This is my dream." He frowned and surveyed their surroundings once again. "How can it be my dream if I've never been here before?"

"You're not making any sense," she countered, her tone low and sumptuous as if a spell had been woven into the words.

She must be imagining things.

"I'm sorry," he rubbed his temple. "My thoughts feel... fuzzy."

So did hers.

The ocean danced calmly around them, and maybe Mera was losing her mind, but she could swear the waves hitting the shore were singing. A sweet, lazy lullaby that scrambled with her common sense. Like the ocean was ensnaring them with a song, only to drown them later, and devour them piece by piece.

A mischievous grin flashed on Bast lips, so white that it stood out against the darkness. He seemed drunk and slightly drowsy.

"I wonder what we should do with this dream." His nostrils flared as he stepped closer. His body's warmth emanated into Mera's, and he laid both hands on her naked hips. "You're so beautiful..."

Mera peeked down at his crotch, that wonderful part of him half-hidden underneath the surface. She wished she could see it... touch it.

Her mind felt like it had shattered into a million pieces, and she had no clue how to pick them up again. She shook her head, trying to focus.

"We need to run," she whispered, her consciousness split in half.

"Why?"

"I don't know. The night is ours." Her words didn't feel like her own. They echoed through the waves, reverberating around the landscape and into Mera's bones.

Her siren grinned, spreading underneath her skin.

She gasped in a panic. The ocean's song, its voice; it was Mera's own!

Poseidon in the trenches, her siren was singing to them both, thickening their thoughts, and freeing their most primal urges.

That bastard! Somehow, she'd brought Bast here, into her dream.

But how?

'Bast has mind powers,' the ocean replied. 'I'm simply tapping into his magic a little.'

Why?

Mera tried to understand her siren's logic, which was her own logic in the end. Deep down, she already knew the answer; she just didn't want to face it.

'Look at him.'

She knew better than to follow her siren's order, but it was too late. The moment she stared into his soft smile, his gaze adoring her with a certain reverence, the remaining common sense she had abandoned her altogether.

"Come to me, kitten." He whispered, brushing a hand over her cheek.

Stepping closer, Mera licked his strong chest.

He inhaled sharply.

Bast tasted of salt and sweat, as fresh as the night sky. A moan escaped her as she stood on the tips of her toes and licked the curve of his neck.

"You should go," she managed, fighting against the urge to kiss him. The urge the song instilled in her skin, straight into her core. The urge she couldn't hold for much longer.

"I'm not going anywhere," he countered before cupping her cheeks.

Mera couldn't tell if this was his real wish or her siren's. It bothered her for a second, but then worry vanished from her mind, the way autumn leaves blow away in the wind.

She took in the scent at the curve of his neck, her fingers digging into his hair. "I need to fuck you, Sebastian Dhay. Desperately."

Bast blinked, something wild and untamed taking over his eyes, and he wrapped strong arms around her waist, bringing her to him.

Mera draped her arms over his shoulders, and together, they danced slowly to the ocean's melody.

Her siren's song.

"I want to fuck you too, Mera," he whispered in her ear, his massive erection pressing into her belly. The tip of his length peeked out of the water, rubbing against her skin. "I've wanted to do it since the moment I laid eyes on you."

Was that the truth or was it the siren speaking for him?

She had no clue. She didn't care.

Mera felt like her body had split in two, the Mera with common sense screaming from a far distance... 'Wake up!'

She wouldn't, of course. Her need for Bast was greater than her resilience. Greater than the entire world.

Her thoughts dizzying, she looked up at him. "Be with me."

He pressed his lips to Mera's, pulling her to him with a certain desperation, his fingers digging into her skin.

They kissed so hard and for so long that she couldn't feel her lips anymore. Their mouths, teeth, tongues, they were caught up in a frenzied war of their own, their breaths shallow and mingled.

When he slightly pulled away, Mera clawed at the base of his neck, begging for his return.

"So eager." He pushed Mera near a smooth faced rock and lifted her up, so her legs crossed around him.

"I need you," she whispered.

The siren's power stole common sense from them both. Or maybe, it freed something that had always been there from day one.

Mera barely registered the bitter possibility that Bast might not feel this way. That perhaps, she was holding him against his will.

The siren chortled at the thought.

'Go on...' The ocean sang to them.

Her arms curled around his shoulders, her legs tightening around him in a clear signal to continue. The space between her thighs yearned for him.

Bast stared at Mera as he entered her with one powerful shove. A loud gasp escaped her lips, but he kept staring at her as he pushed deeper... and deeper.

He clenched his teeth and hissed.

She'd been with other landriders before, Mera had hazy memories of it, but this one was simply extraordinary, his size painfully delirious.

He violently rocked in and out of her, the friction making Mera's mind spin. Deeper he went, his rhythm breaking that of the waves as his tongue invaded her mouth.

Bast was relentless and unmerciful. She moaned loudly as she *lost her sense of self, going higher and higher until she sensed her apex coming.*

A shy squeal broke through her lips.

This was wrong; so wrong. And she didn't want it to stop.

"Mera, fuck!" he growled, burying his head at the curve of her neck.

His rhythm increased. He throbbed inside her, completely ensnared, and so was she. On they went, each other's doom and salvation, a battle of lust and madness that she hoped would last forever.

Fire built inside and Mera burned; no, she blazed.

His name burst from her throat, once, twice. Her body quivered in her undoing, but Bast held her tightly in place. Her limbs clenched against his strong, warm touch, as a glorious dizziness took over her.

"Oh, kitten," he breathed her nickname as if it was a prayer. A part of him exploded into her violently, increasing her own release, and Mera saw stars ahead, above, stars everywhere.

Slowly, she came to herself. Her breathing steadied, but she kept her legs tightly wrapped around him. Caressing his white hair, she whispered, "That was phenomenal, Detective."

Bast was still inside her, pulsing against her walls. "You're mine," he claimed raggedly, his chest heaving as he cupped her cheeks, his thumb running lazily over her bottom lip. "I claim you, Mera Maurea. I claim you under the moon and stars; I claim you under the night sky."

Mera woke with a gasp. She sat up on the bed, glaring at the dark room with light-blue walls.

The sheets and mattress were drenched in her sweat. It clung to her skin and her clothes, the fabric moist and sticky. Her panties, however, were drenched with something else entirely.

The door to the room slammed open suddenly, and she

nearly jumped out of bed. There he stood, outlined by moon-light, a bewildered look on his face.

Maybe Mera was still dreaming.

"What the fuck was that?" Bast demanded.

Cold sweat beaded on her skin. "W-what?"

He pointed to her forehead. "You know what!" Rushing forward, he sat beside her on the bed, with searching eyes that seemed to glow in the darkness.

Only then did she realize he wasn't wearing a shirt.

Lowering his gaze to her chest, he grinned. "Hmm, sweat befits you." He shook his head. "Sorry. I don't know what is happening to me."

The siren's song hadn't completely left him. It hadn't left her, either.

"Bast." She closed her arms over her chest. "We shared that dream, didn't we?"

He nodded. "I have no clue—"

"You have mind powers," she reminded, dragging herself farther from him on the bed. She couldn't let him connect this to her siren; she couldn't allow him to know.

He stared at her, his mouth hanging open. "Mera, I would never—" He swallowed dry. "I have no clue what the fuck just happened. I promise."

Yeah, because she knew who was responsible for this.

Her horny siren.

They sat in the dark for a long, in silence.

"I'm sorry," he offered, his tone strained, his gaze lost and frightened. "I don't know how I did it. Maybe I wanted it badly enough to…" His voice broke.

"Don't be sorry," she blurted as guilt tore her from inside. Though she knew she shouldn't, Mera scooted closer to him and took his hand. "Whatever happened, I wanted it. Did you want it, too?"

Poseidon in the trenches, what if he said no? What if her siren had taken him against his will?

He gave her a wicked grin. "Kitten, I'd have to be crazy not to want it."

Her shoulders relaxed and she let out a deep breath, slamming a hand on her forehead. "Okay. Okay. This is good," she muttered.

She wished she could kill that ravenous force inside her. What if Bast found out she was a waterbreaker? What if he realized Mera had been the one leading the dance?

"So, we both wanted it." His face suddenly lit up. "Did you enjoy it?"

A furious blush swam up to her cheeks, and she fidgeted with the sheets, pressing them tightly against her chest. "It was a dream, Bast. Whatever happened is over now. Best we forget about it, right?" She didn't wait for him to respond before pointing to the door. "Go back to your sofa. We have a big day ahead of us tomorrow."

Leaning forward, he drew circles over her hand with his finger. "Are you sure?" He nodded down at his boxers, which were soiled with his release. "I'll have to sleep naked tonight anyway…"

'Take him!' her siren demanded.

Okay, so Mera *did* want to push Bast against the mattress, pull down his boxers, and take him inside her, but the little common sense she had left stopped her.

'I doubt you would regret it,' her siren countered.

Shut up, you reckless asshole!

"Y-yes," Mera stammered. "I'm sure."

"You don't sound sure, kitten." He observed her for a while, giving her a chance to reconsider.

"Bast, what did you tell me near the end?" she asked, trying to remember it.

"I claim you under the moon and stars. I claim you under the night sky..."

His eyes widened, the lust in them quickly replaced with absolute horror, and a shudder ran down his body. He looked away. "It was just a dream." His focus lingered on the empty space ahead for a while. "You're right, we should rest."

Bast moved to get out of bed, but stopped midway, turning to face her.

"One last thing, though." He leaned closer and brushed the tip of his nose on her right cheek, their lips so close that if she turned just a little...

Her heart drummed in her chest madly, until Mera thought she might faint. She could feel the bastard grinning.

"I guarantee you, kitten," he whispered, his breath soft and warm on her skin, "I'm much better in real life."

CHAPTER 13

Bast's precinct occupied half of the only building in Tir Na Nog that resembled the rest of Hollowcliff. With its squared shape and glassy façade, the construction stuck out amidst the city. It reminded Mera of a lone soldier surrounded by enemy forces.

A soldier losing the fight.

The gray marbled hallway and elevators were the spitting image of the ones from back home, but the similarities stopped when the elevator doors opened to the second floor.

"This is your precinct?" she muttered as she stepped into the vast space.

Fae enjoyed the extravagant, but this was... wow.

The walls were made of polished marble; so were the ceiling and floors. Roots sluggishly spread over the stone, and flowers bloomed from their wooden surface. The vines stretched like veins atop skin, as if the entire place was a living, breathing thing.

A hint of cedar and apricot wafted through the air, coming from mahogany desks that looked heavy and carefully carved—nothing even similar to the compressed wood tables they had back at Mera's precinct. Big windows let in enough sunlight to flood the room, giving it a warm and golden atmosphere.

The place resembled more a palace from faerie tales than a police station.

The layout wasn't much different, however. It had a big open space with separate rooms in the corners for meetings and briefings, and an indoor balcony that led to the third floor.

Some detectives rushed in between the desks, heading for the meeting rooms, while others gathered near small fountains that worked as watercoolers. The rest worked at their tables or discussed case files eagerly.

They wore tailored suits similar to Bast's, but their colors varied. Some wore pink shirts and green vests, others a mix of purple and blue, and very few had the common sense to go for black and white. A moss-haired faerie, eating a cupcake in the corner, stood out with a navy shirt and canary suit.

"What do you bring us, Bast?" someone asked from behind, startling her.

Mera turned to see a tall, thin fae with red spiky hair and clear green eyes. He resembled a teenager after a growth spurt, and definitely not someone who belonged in a police department. Still, he wore the same white uniform as Ruth.

"Captain Asherath." Bast greeted the fae with a humble bow of his head, then gestured to Mera. "This is my partner, Detective Mera Maurea."

Captain Asherath bowed his head slightly at her, placing a hand over his heart. "I'm glad to finally meet you. Bast has told me great things about you."

She also bowed, guessing that was how members—or ex-members—of the Autumn Court greeted each other. "Thank you. But how could Bast have told you anything about me? He doesn't have a phone."

Captain Asherath smiled at Bast. "Perceptive, isn't she?"

"Quite." He gave her a roguish grin. "State secret, kitten."

"Forgive him, Detective," Captain Asherath offered. "He's never had a partner before. Sebastian doesn't trust easily." He shook his head the way the Cap did when Mera misbehaved.

Like when Ruth baked a batch of chocolate chip cookies and told Mera to share them with the neighbor's kid, but instead, she ate them all. It's how she'd gotten her little nickname, actually.

Cookie.

"You see," he went on, "certain Sidhe have the ability to communicate with each other from a distance. Sometimes, we even catch glimpses of the other party's surroundings, or sense how they're feeling—as long as they wish to share such things, of course. It takes weeks for us to create a mind link, but once it's stablished, it works better than one of your phones." He tapped his temple. "Unfortunately, it only covers short distances. If Bast went back to Lunor Insul, I doubt he'd be able to communicate with me."

Lunor Insul. The night fae island.

Given the heavy magic in the waters, the same magic that kept the merfolk away, mobile phones probably wouldn't work either. Something about wavelength interference and whatnot.

Captain Asherath nodded to the desks around them, each with a landline phone that seemed made out of wood. She'd completely missed them at first, since they blended with the desks so stealthily.

"As you can see, we're open to technology. In our own way, that is. Bast and I might communicate through safer methods, and our precinct might be different from the rest of the boroughs, but we're here to protect Hollowcliff at any cost, same as you." He leaned forward. "Just don't tell that to the light courts," he whispered.

Mera smiled. At least this Captain had a sense of humor. She couldn't remember the last time Ruth made a joke.

Why did Captain Asherath communicate with Bast through his mind, though? Either they were hiding something, or they wanted to keep information safe.

She'd find out which soon enough.

"Like most humans, Mera has a talent for pre-judgement," Bast remarked from beside her, earning an immediate shove from her elbow.

Captain Asherath laughed. "Oh, you can keep him in place, Detective Maurea. I never thought Bast could play nice with other kids, but here we are."

"He's not exactly nice." She scoffed.

"He has his moments." Captain Asherath looked around, then motioned for them to follow him into his office.

A lion's head was carved on the door, and wild flowers grew from its mouth. The door must be enchanted like the rest of this place, which meant it must've cost a freaking fortune. Meanwhile, Ruth's office door was the standardized wooden square with a glass panel engraved with her title.

The differences weren't fair, but as Julian had said, Tir Na Nog police got privileges the rest of Tagrad didn't. All because of their magic. Their money, too. After all, the fae state was the richest in Tagrad.

At some point, though, this had to stop. A civil war had never felt closer than it did right now.

Inside, Captain Asherath's office was an exact copy of Ruth's, down to the bookshelves lining the wall behind a leather chair, and the carefully carved mahogany table facing the door. It was a relief. At least here, there were no privileges.

A white leather sofa rested across the left wall, the single difference between both offices—the Cap's was brown.

Asherath closed the heavy door and sat on his chair,

facing them. His easy manner disappeared, his expression growing somber and ridiculously similar to Ruth's. "Before you report on your visit to the Summer King's home, I want to run something by you." He stared directly at Bast.

"Shoot."

"Have you considered that whoever wants you dead might not be linked to the case?"

A heavy silence filled the room.

"That seems unlikely," Mera jumped in. "If they're not linked to the case, why go after Bast right now? The witch said a seer predicted Bast would kill someone, and that this someone hired her. It has to be our culprit, right?"

Asherath nodded. "You have a point, Detective. However, Bast informed me the witch didn't want *you* dead. If whoever is behind this intended to mess with the investigation, they would've tried to kill two birds with one stone, and get rid of *both* detectives working the case, don't you think?"

He was right.

Asherath may seem soft and sweet, but he was Captain for a reason.

"It's not impossible, I guess." Bast ran a hand through his hair. "I've put some power-heavy Sidhe in prison, and my solve rate is the highest in the precinct. The light courts were bound to come after me sooner or later. But Mera is right. Why now?"

The captain raised his shoulders. "No idea. But Zev Ferris' killer is calculating. They drowned Sara Hyland and used her as bait. That points to someone cold and cruel." He nodded to Mera. "Would someone like that take action based on a feeble vision?"

His reasoning left her in awe. Fae weren't exactly famous for logical thinking, but Asherath's was spot on about the case.

"Anyway." He extended his hand to her. "I believe you had something for me?"

She nodded, pulling the plastic bag with the phone from the inside pocket of her jacket. "This belonged to Zev Ferris."

His green eyes widened. "Did it?" He whistled lowly as he studied the device. "A king from a light court owning a phone. Now, I've seen everything." Laying it on his wooden table, he leaned back in his chair, forming a circle with his hands. "Is that why Lisandra Ferris dropped by my office to make an official complaint?"

That sneaky bitch!

Bast stepped forward. "Fallon, she—"

"I can handle Lisandra. But you left her apartment yesterday, and you're handing me this phone now."

Bast clicked his tongue and shrugged. "Traffic was a bitch."

"Right." There was no humor in the Captain's tone. "And you conveniently forgot that you have wings. And that you could even winnow, if you put your mind to it?"

The wicked, yet childlike grin Bast gave him was a thing of wonder. "I'm a lazy bastard, Fallon."

Captain Asherath let out an exasperated breath. "Fine. I'll hand the phone to the guys over for analysis."

"To Redford, yes? Directly to his hands." Bast's tone weighed boulders.

"Of course, to Redford." Asherath's forehead crinkled. "I'm not an idiot, Sebastian. Laula and Guli are on Summer's payroll and everyone knows it."

It was strange seeing the two police officers, one of them a freaking Captain, having to tip-toe around the corruption in their own department.

"Go on, then." Asherath swooshed them away. "Time is of the essence."

As soon as they left the precinct, Mera turned to Bast. "Your Captain is pretty cool."

"Cool isn't the right word." He chuckled. "Relentless might be better. Fallon is one of the few whom I trust in there." Bast shoved his hands in his pockets and watched the sandstone pebbles at his feet. "I'm surprised an honest fae like him has lasted this long."

"I'm not. He's resourceful." She laid a gentle hand on his shoulder. "Smart, too. I can see your Captain keeping his title for a long time."

He gave her a tight-lipped smile, heavy with worry. "I hope you're right."

Turning ahead, Mera watched the wide street, where Sidhe zinged about in straight lines, either boosted by magic or their wings.

Some wore elaborated and colorful dresses that should belong to a museum, others had modern and practical clothes such as jeans and jumpers. A few wore fighting leathers, and a great many sported magical fabrics that resembled rustling leaves or flowing water.

'We need one of those,' her siren muttered in awe.

It's completely see-through!

'Exactly.'

A wooden bus packed with trolls, pixies, and banshees drove sluggishly across the street. The Sidhe flew around and over it, since they were much faster than the vehicle, but Mera could hardly keep up with it all. The fae moved like shooting stars and zinging bees.

She pointed to the traffic—if one could call it that. "Did you know Clifftown and Lycannie are working on a machine that can fly? I've heard it has wings."

Bast blew air through his lips. "Come on, kitten."

"I'm serious!"

He rolled his eyes, but seemed to ponder. "Considering

what your technology has done so far, I wouldn't call it impossible. Maybe you'll join us in the sky soon enough."

A fuzzy and warm sensation filled her chest, which didn't make much sense. Humans might not be Mera's people, but they were the only people she had left. She took pride in their accomplishments as if they were her own.

"It will happen, Bast. You'll see."

She always imagined flying might be akin to swimming in the ocean's currents; the same currents she would never feel on her skin again. Mera couldn't return to the sea, but the sky above waited for her. "Whenever this machine is ready, I'll be the first to go for a ride."

He frowned. "But you already know what flying feels like."

"I was unconscious when you took me to Stella, remember?"

"Good point." He gave her a lazy, sideways grin. "Call me surprised. Air isn't exactly your element."

It wasn't the air, specifically, but the currents that she craved.

"Oh, really?" She crossed her arms. "And what *is* my element?"

He smirked but didn't reply.

A heavy, trembling sensation settled in her stomach.

"All right, then." Bast's mighty gray wings spread out of thin air, and flapped. He hovered inches above ground, offering her his hand. "If you insist."

Mera gasped, exhilaration spinning inside her. "Seriously?"

Instead of answering, he hooked his arms underneath hers, and boosted, going higher and higher.

Mera screamed louder than a child riding their first rollercoaster. Her feet dangled as she watched the streets and buildings shrinking below. Panic set in her stomach, but it also fueled her.

Faster and higher they went, and as Bast took her in loops and straight lines, Mera became... *free*.

Free like she hadn't been since she'd left the ocean. Flying wasn't different from swimming after all.

'I could get used to this,' her siren cheered.

Loud huzzahs and laughter burst from her lips as Bast zinged with her into the deep blue.

"This is amazing!" she yelled, utterly carefree.

"Of course it is!" Bast shouted over the howling wind, and she noticed he was smiling, too.

They went on for what could've been hours but felt like minutes, until Bast landed them atop a terracotta building.

He panted discreetly, as if trying to hide the effort.

Mera's head spun from all the loops. She tried to balance on her own two feet, but ended up leaning against Bast to gain her footing.

She looked up at him, watching the bewildered strings of hair that had escaped his bun. It seemed as if an electric current had jolted straight through him.

"You don't look much different." He pointed at her messy hair as his gray wings disappeared behind him.

Mera didn't care. She'd loved flying. Having her hair form a cuckoo's nest atop her head had been totally worth it.

Sunset drenched everything around them in a soft, warm glow, turning Bast into nothing short of a vision. The orange hue that swallowed the world reflected in his eyes.

"Thank you," she said, her voice hoarse and heavy. "I loved it."

His hand brushed the back of her waist, his eyes curious and expecting. "Did you?" Leaning forward, he nudged the tip of his nose with hers. "What else did you enjoy?"

"I..."

His grip on her waist strengthened and he pulled her closer to him. "Do you love this?"

Poseidon in the trenches, she could feel his chest heaving up and down against hers, the warmth of his skin, and the hardness of his muscles. It was like she'd entered a trance. Like Bast was the siren, and Mera the sailor lost at sea.

"Yes," she whispered. "I love this, too."

He brushed a stray lock of hair from her temple, then cupped her cheek. "Mera, I…"

His ears twitched and his eyes widened before he pushed her away and jumped back. Just in time to escape the silver dagger that tore through the space he occupied not a second ago.

CHAPTER 14

THE FAE WATCHED them with feral yellow eyes, two ambers that burned along with the sunset. He was clad in black fighting leathers, the belts wrapped around his chest and waist packed with daggers, knives, and tiny weapons shaped like obsidian stars with sharp edges.

Another assassin.

Bast cracked his neck left and right. "Mera, take cover."

Instead, she pulled out her gun and aimed at the faerie. "The hell I will."

Their opponent gave them a cruel grin, before unsheathing a long sword from his belt. Fully ignoring Mera, he pointed it at Bast, even if she was about to use his head as a shooting target.

"Brother of shadows, today you must die," he said.

At least he had the courtesy of speaking English.

His skin was the color of bark, and his short, spikey hair was purple, even though he seemed to belong to the Night court. A long white scar ran from his left eyebrow down to his chin.

Bast raised his shoulders. "That's what the last assassin said, *malachai*."

Mera had learned the word during a beer-pong game in college. It basically meant *motherfucker*, it just sounded prettier.

"The witch was weak. I am not." Purple flames burst from the bounty hunter's hand and ran through his blade.

"Move and you're dead," Mera warned.

"Iron bullets won't stop him," Bast explained without looking at her, his attention solely on their opponent. "Go take cover, or I swear—"

"No way. You're my partner, at least for the time being." She tightened her grip on the gun. "Iron bullets might not stop this assface, but they'll sure as hell slow him down."

"This isn't your battle, Mera," Bast snapped.

As fast as lightning, the bounty hunter grabbed one of his pointy stars and flung it toward her. Mera blinked, too late realizing she might be dead.

To her own surprise, she kept breathing. One of the weapon's pointy edges had hit the gun's muzzle, blocking it.

"What the…" She showed it to Bast. "What is this thing? I thought you guys didn't like metal."

"It's a Shileken. And that's not metal."

Mera yanked the weapon out of her gun, analyzing the smooth, obsidian surface. "It's… stone?" Stone cut so sharply, it bit into the tip of her finger. Throwing it aside, she kept her weapon aimed at the faerie. "Better not miss next time, you monumental shit twat."

Bast rolled his eyes and flicked his hand. An invisible force pushed Mera straight into the building's main shaft, gluing her to the red surface. It felt smooth as clay and hard as cement.

She tried to move, but the seamless power increased the more she fought it. "Bast, you son of a—"

"You should have taken cover, kitten." His tone was bored and nonchalant. He turned to the assassin and closed his fists. "Shall we?"

"I'll take care of your human later." His lips curled in disgust as he eyed Mera up and down. "A Night Prince consorting with a human... what a shame."

"Well, fuck you, too," she snapped. "And we'll see who takes care of who, *malachai*."

The bounty hunter fixed his battle stance and raised his sword at Bast. "Your human has a dirty mouth."

Mera pushed against Bast's magic, but it didn't yield. "Let me out!" She still held her gun, but with her hand slammed against the wall, she couldn't take aim.

'Use the macabre,' her siren whispered. *'Or sing to them, make them kneel to your every whim...'*

Mera couldn't do that without revealing her true nature.

The assassin boosted toward Bast, but her partner was faster. He jumped back in a loop as the faerie rushed forward, then kicked him in the spine, sending the asshole toppling over the building's ledge.

The bounty hunter slammed the tip of his flaming sword on the ridge and swung around, landing on his own two feet at the last minute.

Bast peered at him. "Who sent you?"

The faerie wielded his sword, bellowing a war cry as he ran toward Bast. Her partner clicked his tongue and winced, as if the assassin was a nuisance no greater than a bug.

Darkness pulsed from Bast's body, rising from his skin and concentrating on two spheres of void that swirled atop his hands. He shot both at the mercenary, who flung one away with a swing of his magical sword.

The other hit him straight in the gut.

The fae kept his screams in his throat, but veins popped

on his forehead, his eyes glistening as he struggled to keep standing.

The reek of burnt leather and flesh wafted in the air.

Bast retied his messy hair into a neat bun as he strolled toward the wounded fae. "Brother from the shadows, you know who I am and what I can do." He studied the assassin with curiosity. "And still, you defy me. I can't decide if you're mad or stupid."

The bounty hunter grunted as he forced himself straight, putting most of his weight on his sword. Beads of sweat peppered his skin, his muscles clenched. A circle of singed leather and flesh marred his stomach.

"You left us, *brother*. You left because you are weak." He launched himself at Bast.

Her partner lifted his arm and a thin layer of darkness blinked out of thin air, a shield made of night and stars. It met the sword with the loud clank of metal hitting metal, but there were no sparks.

The mercenary tried to remove the sword from the shield, but it was stuck. Tentacles of night rose from the darkness, wrapping around the tip of the blade. Black rust spread through the metal, infecting it like a disease, until there was nothing left but ashes.

The bounty hunter cursed in Faeish, letting go of the handle before the rust got to his hand. Faster than Bast could react, the fae whirled around and broke through his defense.

The bastard jabbed at his rib, then punched his face.

Bast's shield disappeared into thin air.

The assassin had the upper hand and he wouldn't stop. Purple flames burst from his closed fist as he sucker-punched Bast's stomach so furiously he flung him away.

Her partner landed harshly on the floor, his body skidding over the concrete.

"Let me out!" Mera pushed herself against Bast's spell, but his magic was too strong.

He groaned and winced, as if something other than the bounty hunter's attack was hurting him. When Mera stopped struggling, Bast's body immediately relaxed, which meant that every time she fought against his magic, she fought against Bast himself.

He couldn't afford the distraction.

He gave her a weak, thankful smile as he forced himself to his feet. "I've got this, kitten." The front of his vest and shirt were completely singed, showcasing his muscular abs. His skin was a little red around the wound, but it wasn't filled with bubbles like his opponent's.

Mera sighed in relief.

The assassin removed a dagger from one of his belts and licked it. "Night Prince, I expected more."

"Seers are a sham," Bast stated, steadying himself into a battle stance. "If you're working for someone who believes in visions, you're pathetic."

"Their money is as good as anyone else's, though I wouldn't know. I'm not charging for your hit." He played with his dagger, spinning it around his hand.

That was odd. No mercenary worth their two cents would ever do a job for free, and the asshole was a pro, as much as Mera hated admitting it.

"A bounty hunter without a bounty? Now I've seen everything," Bast replied without amusement.

"The seer who foretold my employer's doom was Karthana. Do you understand me now, my prince?"

Bast dropped his fists, his jaw hanging open. "Impossible."

The assassin took advantage of his shock and ran at him again, grabbing another dagger from his belt.

Something in Bast changed. Tentacles of void sprouted from his skin, and fluttering flames of night rose around him like a bonfire. Pitch-black filled every corner of his eyes.

That wasn't Bast anymore. It was the monster from the train wreck.

"At last, the death bringer arrives!" The assassin's eyes turned fully purple as he ran, his fangs growing bigger and sharper.

Bast didn't have daggers to fight back, even a gun or a sword. Nothing but his night and stars.

It wasn't fair.

The two clashed violently, but Bast avoided the cuts and charges from the bounty hunter with ease. His night tentacles tried to wrap around the fae's limbs, but the assassin was fast. His purple flames whipped at Bast's leg, making a cut on his gray pants that showed a reddish patch of skin.

In return, Bast's flames slammed on his right arm, leaving a torn sleeve and a red, bubbling line on their path.

Their magic fought like they did, brutally and without mercy.

Bast dodged one dagger swing, grabbed the bounty hunter's fist, and punched the bastard's elbow from the outside, breaking the bone. It stuck out from his skin, the same way the half of a sinking ship sticks out of water.

Mera winced at the sight.

The dagger fell to the floor. The assassin barely had time to scream before Bast swiveled around, grabbed his other wrist and punched his left elbow.

The second dagger clanked against the ground, joining its twin.

The fae bellowed as he fell to his knees, his teeth clenched. "*Rae-henai, baku!*"

Certain words in Faeish meant entire sentences. If Mera recalled correctly, "*Rae-henai*" translated to something akin to "I curse you forever."

Yeah, fae had a penchant for the dramatic☐and for cursing.

Taking one of the daggers from the floor, Bast played with it, spinning it in circles.

"Who sent you?" he asked again, stepping closer.

"I'll never tell!"

Bast shrugged, and with one swift move, cut off the faerie's left ear. The bounty hunter held his screams through clenched teeth.

"How about now?"

"Bast, stop!" Mera yelled, but her partner was gone, replaced by this bloodthirsty beast. "Let's cuff him and take him down to the station!"

Tears formed in the bounty hunter's purple eyes. A surge of his magic snapped at Bast, but her partner's night tentacles slapped it away, before disappearing underneath his skin.

"I'll ask again," Bast warned. "Who sent you?"

When the assassin stayed silent, Bast cut off his remaining ear as if he were slicing a piece of steak.

Mera closed her eyes, but the sound of the blade slowly cutting flesh and cartilage was too loud, even if muffled by the faerie's horrid screams.

Everyone knew that cutting a fae's ear brought great shame upon them. Taking two seemed beyond cruel.

"Bast!" she called once he was done. "This isn't you!"

"Oh, no, Mera." He grinned wide at her, like a demon in the horror movies the Cap forbade her to watch when she was young. He threw the bleeding ear on the floor, like he was giving her a trophy. "There's no running from myself."

Bast turned and crouched, placing the belly of the dagger below his opponent's chin. He lifted the tip of the blade, straining the fae's neck.

"Shall we try a third time?"

"Maim me all you want. I'm sworn to the bounty." Sweat

mingled with the assassin's tears, his teeth clenched. "Let me live in shame, *brother*, and I'll come back for you. I'll come for your human, too."

Fear, cold and ruthless, gnawed at Mera's chest. The faerie was goading Bast into killing him, and there was only one way to stop it.

"Detective Dhay, I'm placing you under arrest right now!"

"No, you're not," he countered without turning to her. "I can make this quick, brother of shadows. Just tell me what I need to know."

The faerie gave him a mad laugh. "The king is dead. Long live the king."

Bast stopped for a moment, his eyes widening. His expression became suddenly cold, merciless, and for the first time since they'd met, Mera truly feared him.

A freezing chill swam down her spine. "Bast, please," she mumbled.

He didn't listen, instead, he kept the tip of the dagger pressed against the assassin's neck, his pitch-black eyes flat. "You leave me no choice."

He thrust the blade forward.

CHAPTER 15

Somewhere in the past...

ONLY LANDRIDERS without any magic inhabited the Isles of Fog, which was why they lacked forbidden zones around their territory.

These landriders—Professor Currenter called them *humans*—weren't like the ones living in the continent. They didn't have guns or electric fields. They led a rudimentary life, without the technology Mother so loved, the same technology she claimed one day would take Atlanteans back to land.

The islanders lived in huts or in the forests, communing with the nature around them. They also worshipped water-breakers as their deities, which seemed silly to her.

"Why are we here, Mother?" she asked as she stood in the water beside the queen. The calm waves brushed past Mera's waist and covered her mother up to her thighs. Mera could barely see the shore through the thick fog. "Can we go back? I'm supposed to train with Professor Currenter today."

"We are here to take sacrifice," the queen snapped, then focused on the beach, where four figures stood watching them, their forms blurry through the heavy mist.

The isles certainly deserved their name.

Mother opened her mouth and started singing a melodic, beautifully cruel tune. Soon enough, one of the figures stepped into the water and approached them.

A landrider stood before the queen. He was bigger than her, and his body looked as if it was made of stones. He simply stood there, entranced as he watched her with a foolish grin, adoration shining from his dazed brown eyes. "You're so beautiful…"

Queen Ariella's teeth turned sharp and pointy, which meant she was about to feed. She licked her lips and ran her hands through the human's strong shoulders, chest and stomach, then addressed Mera without paying her any attention. "I've changed my mind, weakling. Poseidon has granted me a remarkable male… You will not witness sacrifice today. Go home."

"Alone?" She observed the way they'd come—which was the entire ocean ahead—and shook. "What if I get lost?"

The queen rolled her eyes. "I intend to have fun with this one before eating it, so go home. Now!" she snarled when Mera didn't move.

Mera couldn't hold the sob that came out, or the cries that followed. She was barely a merling; she hadn't braved the vast ocean on her own—it could be a scary place, even for a grown-up. Returning home alone might as well be her doom. "Mother, please…"

The queen grabbed her arms, her nails digging into Mera's skin enough to draw blood. "What did I teach you? Say it!"

"T-the royal bloodline doesn't cry." She sniffed, feeling warm water trickling down her cheeks.

Tears. Mera had only cried underwater, so she didn't know how they felt as the drops strolled down her skin, sliding down the edges of her mouth. But these were tears, she knew it because Professor Currenter said they tasted salty.

Maybe the ocean was made of waterbreaker tears.

"I'm scared," she croaked.

"You should be scared, but not of the ocean." The queen rubbed her temples. "Fine." She took the man's hand and sunk into the water.

Mera followed.

Her mother plummeted ahead with the human, who kept smiling as bubbles left his nostrils and mouth.

"He'll die, Mother!"

"That's the point." She didn't turn to Mera as she kept sinking. "I wish for landrider flesh today and that's what I shall have."

Mera had heard about the sacrifices. Only royals had the permission to claim them, but few actually did it. As Professor Currenter once said, *"We're not savages, dear."*

Was her mother a savage, then?

Mera stopped midway, watching the human's body begin to thrash. Terror broke through the spell, and he stretched his free hand to her, silently begging for his life.

She should hate landriders. They'd hunted down and cast away waterbreakers from their rightful place on land. Atlantea used to be split into two cities; one of land and one of sea.

Now there was only the sea.

Mother hated landriders with a fury, and so should Mera, but this human was innocent. He was an islander who'd never set foot in the continent. Besides, Queen Ariella hated a world of things, not all of them worthy of her wrath; Mera being the best example.

She doubted her little heart had enough space for Mother's infinite rage.

That landrider wouldn't meet his end in the heat of battle or as an old man; the two "best ways to go" according to Professor Currenter. He would die to become food, like the sharks, fish, and whales waterbreakers ate for sustenance.

Was there any difference, though?

Flesh was flesh. And yet, what her mother was about to do felt... wrong. Wrong enough, that in a pulse, Mera summoned the water in the ocean, letting its magic flow into her veins.

She couldn't understand what she was doing, but she and the ocean became one, and they were strong, and they were free. She moved her arms in oval shapes, commanding the water to form a maelstrom that pushed the human to the surface.

Queen Ariella wasn't expecting it, so she couldn't stop the whirlpool that had already shot the man up, and back to his island.

"What have you done, weakling?" her mother asked through grinding teeth.

Whatever courage had possessed Mera vanished in an eye blink, and by the rage in the queen's face, she might die today.

Mother didn't give her time to explain or beg for mercy. She shot the macabre toward her, and Mera's blood thrashed in her own veins. She writhed underneath her own skin, being pulled in different directions from the inside out.

She couldn't breathe right; the pain was so grand she could barely focus. "Mommy, no!" she cried.

It all suddenly stilled. The pain waned and Mera took in long gulps of water through her gills.

"The next time you call me 'mommy' I'll kill you." The queen swam forward, facing Mera. "You're lucky I want my hands dirty today."

Holding Mera by the neck, she punched her face. The ocean spun around her and she could barely register the next punch, and the next.

Mother kneed her stomach next, and Mera bent over. The following hit went to her spine, then her face again.

Mera's frail body would soon break, but she welcomed the peace and quiet of death. No more endless beatings, no more glares of anger and contempt.

Just… silence.

Sharp nails ripped Mera's chest as darkness crept through the edges of her vision. The queen went on and on, punching and clawing, until Mera couldn't feel the strikes anymore.

Mommy was going to kill her.

No, mommy had already killed her.

And then everything went black.

Mera woke in Professor Currenter's cave, lying in a hole carved into the stone wall of his living room. Glowing yellow algae glued to the ceiling shed dim light on her. It reminded Mera of a starry sky.

The professor was attending to her wounds, pulling the magic from the water into glittering blue whisps of light that penetrated her cuts and bruises.

Her tiny body didn't hurt anymore, so he must be numbing her pain.

"Professor?" She blinked, centering herself. "What happened? Where's Mother?"

The old waterbreaker laid a gentle hand on her forehead. There in the vast deep, things didn't float so easily, so Mera could relax atop the smooth rock surface of the pod.

His white hair was tied in a tight bun behind his head, a reminiscence of his time in the military—all male soldiers fixed their hair that way. He also wore those uncomfortable scaled fabrics Mother called pants, the cobalt scales matching the hue of his skin.

"Don't ever defy the queen again, Mera," he quietly pleaded as he willed the water's magic into her. "Promise me."

"But she was going to kill that human."

"She kills for sport. She kills for hunger. She kills and kills." His hands shook as he cupped her cheeks. "Do not repeat your brothers and sisters' mistake. Do not defy her, little fry. I can't lose you, too."

"I had brothers and sisters?" Mera gasped.

"It doesn't matter now. They're in the past."

Mera opened her mouth to ask a million questions, but the professor stopped her.

"Knowing about them won't bring them back. They're forever gone. You'll follow their path if you keep challenging her."

"But you taught me to fight for what's right," she countered, feeling the magic bring back her strength. "What Mommy... *Mother* did, wasn't right."

Sorrow overcame his face. "You can't go against her, Mera. You're not strong enough."

She took that in, a bitter taste flowing down her throat. "It's not fair."

"It's the truth."

Crossing her arms, she sat up, leaning over her knees. He stopped willing magic into her and waited.

"Why doesn't she love me?"

"The queen loves no one." He lifted her chin gently. "But you don't need her love to be happy, do you?"

Mera honestly couldn't say. Even though her existence was an unbearable string of miserable events, thanks to the queen, a silly part of her craved for the love that wasn't there. And yet, if she had to choose between having the queen's love or Professor Currenter's, she would choose him every single time.

He was her mentor, her confidant, and once Mera prayed he were her progenitor, especially after hearing rumors about his *entanglement* with her mother—though she had no clue what said entanglement meant, or how it generated offspring.

Yet, when Mera asked him, he had denied it. *"The queen takes what the queen wills, even if one's preference does not lie with the opposite gender,"* he'd said quietly then, his tone shaking with grief. *"There's nothing in the world I'd love more than to call you my seed, but that you are not, my dear princess."*

In any case, Mera loved him a lot more than she did Mother—which to Queen Ariella's own credit, wasn't tremendously hard.

The professor tapped his chin and narrowed his eyes at her. "You seem fit enough for one class. What do you say, little fry?"

"Keep at it," Professor Currenter ordered as he strolled atop the ocean's surface.

Today the sea was calm and placid, nearly as straight as land.

"It's hard!" Mera winced as she forced the water beneath her feet to push her up, while the force the Professor called gravity pulled her down. The scaled clothes that clung to her skin were sticky and uncomfortable. "Why do I have to wear this?"

"Your mother's best scientists came up with these body-suits," he reminded her. "Pray that the queen doesn't hear you dismissing their finds."

"They're silly," she grumbled. "I'm much more comfortable naked."

"Aren't we all? But this fabric helps tone your muscles, and it eases your breathing on the surface." He pointed to her round ears and the pinkish hue taking over her skin. "We've been up for an hour, and you didn't need to spit out water once in order to breathe air. That's truly remarkable, is it not?"

She hated admitting it, but it was.

"The bodysuits also help us move with ease up here, since the gravity above water is considerably stronger." He patted his own scaled pants. "All in all, not a bad invention."

"If you say so," she muttered under her breath. "But why do I have to learn to walk on water? It's pointless! We live underneath."

"We do, but this is part of your waterbending training." He put both hands behind his back. "Now, surprise me, little fry."

How? She could barely keep standing!

Her head pounded, and her body strained from the effort. This was the price of using magic for too long. Professor Currenter said she had to get used to it, but Poseidon in the trenches, it was hard.

Mera lost her balance, but by waterbending a tiny jet underneath her feet, she quickly regained it.

Fine, then.

Stretching her arm forward, she summoned a small pillar

of water. It swirled up to her palm, bending into curvy shapes. A dolphin, a starfish, then a turtle.

Mera giggled.

"Good," Professor Currenter praised, his stand unwavering atop the ocean's surface. "Control the tiny parts that make the water what it is. Slow down that which makes the liquid."

Mera nodded. The line began solidifying into ice.

"Perfect. You can bend water well enough. Now, bend my blood."

"No!" The ice shattered into pieces that plonked down below, then floated back to the surface. "The macabre scares me."

"You must learn it nonetheless." He tapped his chest, and even though his pinkish skin was slightly flabby, his muscles worn, Mera could spot the mighty soldier he must have been once. "Come on. We don't have all day."

It seemed she didn't have a choice.

Blood was water, so the macabre wasn't much different from waterbending. The only problem was, Professor Currenter's blood, much like Mera's, had magic, and magic fought back against foreign commands.

She wiggled her fingers, feeling the blood coursing through his veins.

"Good. Control it."

Nodding, she tried to speed up the flow, but his vital fluids didn't follow her command.

He was blocking her.

"Will you teach me how to block another's macabre?" Mera asked quietly, the memory of Mother's cruelty still fresh in her mind.

"Soon, my princess. In the meantime, keep trying to break through my barrier."

She frowned and pushed, but she couldn't get her ability

to work, until the power inside her noticed a presence in the distance, like a shark catching the scent of blood. That presence, unlike the professor, wouldn't put up a fight.

The wild force inside her jolted into the horizon, and soon found what it'd been looking for.

Nightbringer.

Panic set in Mera's stomach, but the macabre pushed itself forward, taking a life of its own. She felt the hearts of every landrider in that ship, the flow of their blood. Most didn't have magic, so they were easy prey.

Slowly, she lost her sense of self, her sense of being. It was just the macabre and her; they were one and the same. How interesting it was, to hold so many lives in the palm of her hand.

Was this what Mommy—no, *Mother*—felt during the hundreds of times she'd tried to kill her?

It wasn't unpleasant, really.

Mera remembered the times she'd watched Nightbringers sail from above. The horror at the sight of their sharp harpoons, the spiked hulls that glinted under moonlight, heralding the coming of death. Her mother didn't want to alert landriders to Atlantean technology, which meant her people couldn't fight back.

So they hid. They hid as much as they could. And sometimes, it wasn't enough.

The islanders were innocent, but landriders from the continent were far from that.

One command.

It was all it took.

Mera would pull strings; strings that connected her to every single creature in that ship. Some would choke on their own blood, others might explode from the inside out, and few might survive—if they were strong enough.

Professor Currenter watched her carefully, his arms crossed. "You are your mother's daughter."

A sword piercing through her chest would have hurt less. Mera blinked, realizing what she'd nearly done.

She stepped back on the water and released those blood-soaked strings, praying to Poseidon she'd never hold them again.

"First rule of the macabre, dear," Professor Currenter warned. "Don't let it control you."

"I-I wouldn't," she told herself. "I couldn't!"

"You nearly did." A rush of water beneath his feet pushed him toward her, and he laid a hand over her shoulder. "But you *chose* not to, little fry. That's what truly matters."

"Professor, I didn't mean to—"

"Your choices define you, Mera. The macabre is a mighty power, that if used without reproach can consume its wielder. So be careful."

"Did it consume the queen?" she blurted, not knowing where the thought had originated. "Is that why she lusts for death and misery, every minute of every day?"

"Poseidon's gifts are strong in the Wavestorm bloodline."

That was all he said.

She lowered her head. "Will you help me control these… *gifts?*"

Smiling, he lifted her chin softly. "I will show you how to control them yourself. How about that?"

Mera couldn't thank him enough. Professor Currenter was the light in her darkness, the only being in the entire world who cared for her.

Tears trickled down her cheeks as she wrapped her arms around him and cried. No, she sobbed.

"I don't know what I'd do without you," Mera croaked, fearing for things she couldn't quite understand, things that might never happen.

"My dear princess." He bent over and hugged her, patting her head. "Hush now. I'll always be here, right beside you."

But the old waterbreaker shouldn't have made promises he couldn't keep.

CHAPTER 16

MERA TOOK a small wooden bowl filled with a green paste, and submerged a cloth into it, dabbing the mixture gingerly onto Bast's left eye. The spot was swollen and purpling, but according to him, the paste would make it go away in a matter of hours.

"Stella's secret recipe," he'd explained.

Mera applied the remedy methodically while silence hung around them, heavy as lead.

Bast stared straight ahead, his brow slightly creased with annoyance. "Stop judging me," he finally grumbled.

"I'm not."

"Yes, you are." He lowered her hand, searching for something in her eyes. "I had to kill him, Mera."

"No, you didn't." She put down the bowl and the cloth on the coffee table, near the med kit she'd opened the moment they'd returned to the house. "The assassin wasn't a threat, not after you broke his arms and cut his ears."

Her throat knotted at the memory of the dagger piercing through his neck.

150

They could've talked about their options before Bast killed the fae. Before he grabbed the body and flew away without warning.

They could've discussed it the moment he came back to the house late at night, or as he prepared the paste that Mera was applying to his wounds. But no. He was only ready to talk now.

Prick.

Bast grumbled a curse and turned away, staring at the wall. "You don't know what you're talking about. Injured or not, he was dangerous. He had magic, and he would never stop. He said so himself. I couldn't risk him hurting you."

"Don't pin this on me, partner."

He stared at her, his blue eyes shining with childlike wonder, his tantalizing lips slightly open, almost like he didn't believe what she'd said. It took Mera a moment to realize she'd never called Bast "partner" to his face, and actually meant it.

Maybe she was wrong, or going crazy, but admitting it aloud seemed to make him happy. If that was the case, she'd always call him partner. Even if she was still mad at him.

"You *are* my partner, kitten," he agreed. "It's why I couldn't run the risk. Besides, he was a dead fae walking."

"What do you mean?"

"Assassins like him are magically tied to the bounty. If he didn't finish his task, the magical bind would consume him in a few weeks."

Mera shuddered as she remembered waterbreakers dissolving into ashes when they crossed into the forbidden zone.

Sure, both bounty hunters had attacked first, and maybe killing the second one had been a mercy, but ending their lives was wrong, nonetheless.

Even if it meant saving Bast's and her own?

Taking the bowl, she pushed his chest back onto the sofa, slamming his upper body against the padded surface. "Remove your shirt."

A grin spread on his lips and he promptly unbuttoned what remained of the fabric. He tossed it aside and crossed both arms behind his neck, showing her his strong biceps. "When Danu gives, one does not ask why."

Mera rolled her eyes and dipped the cloth into the bowl. As much as she loved admiring the hard shapes of his body, the circle of red flesh in the middle of his torso glared back at her.

Bast acted as if it was no big deal, but he had to be in serious pain.

When she dabbed the paste atop the wound, his body went stiff. He hissed through his teeth, his hands dropping to his sides and closing into fists.

She stopped, watching him with worry, but he nodded in a go-ahead.

"You can't just kill people," she chided, continuing their conversation. "You're a detective. If we don't follow the code, we're no better than the criminals we're trying to catch."

She sounded like the Cap, and a sense of pride took over, but then Mera remembered that her human façade was nothing more than a shell. That she shouldn't forget her true nature, and who her *true* mother was.

'Never!' She and her siren agreed.

"The guy and the witch tried to kill me," Bast reminded as she applied the remedy, his muscles clenched in pain. "It was self-defense."

"Bullshit." Slowly, his body relaxed. Either he was getting used to the pain, or he couldn't feel it anymore. "If that helps you sleep at night, then whatever. Consider yourself a freaking saint, Bast."

"Hmm, never been called one of your saints before." He scratched his chin. "I could get used to this."

"Dickwart," she grumbled under her breath.

Mera kept dabbing at the big wound until the mixture covered all of it Grabbing a strip of gauze from the med kit on the coffee table, she began wrapping it around his torso.

"It's not just the fact you killed him, Bast," she said, ignoring how close they were as she wrapped the gauze. "It's *how* you killed him."

He shrugged. "Extreme times, extreme measures."

"Is Captain Asherath aware of your *extreme measures*? Does he agree?"

"I haven't been able to contact him yet, but I guess he would," he spoke without a hint of doubt.

"Who's Karthana?" She secured the ends of the gauze with an adhesive strip, finishing her work. "The faerie mentioned Karthana's vision put the bounty on your head."

Bast had become a different fae after hearing that name.

He hunched over his knees, hands intertwined. He winced, having forgotten the huge wound on his stomach, but didn't lean back. "She was my betrothed, once."

Blood drained from Mera's face. Her heart stopped. "You're freaking married?"

"I called off the engagement before I came to the continent." He gave her a sideways grin. "No need to be jealous."

She slapped his arm. "I'm not jealous, *wu baku*."

Translation: you idiot. Being with Bast was certainly improving her language skills.

He snickered. "You enjoy cursing in Faeish, don't you?"

She did, yes, but she didn't tell him.

His chest rose and fell with a heavy breath. "We believe that when royalty has a vision, it's bound to come true. But Karthana wasn't a psychic, and she never had visions. Ever."

"Maybe she had her own motivations. Maybe she's lying."

Which was the most plausible explanation, especially if she resented Bast for leaving. "But why would the assassin do the work for free? Was he related to her?"

Bast scratched the back of his neck. "Kind of. Karthana's father is the head of the League of Darkness, one of the greatest assassins' guilds in Tagrad. That's where the bounty hunter came from. And it would make sense for her father to send the witch before. He was probably testing the waters by using a different guild."

"Mystery solved!" Mera tapped her own legs. "An angry ex-girlfriend. Somehow I'm not surprised."

His forehead crinkled. "Maybe. But if the vision put me in danger, I doubt Karthana would blab. We parted on good terms."

Did they?

A strange, prickling sensation stung her chest.

"Unless, whoever is behind this offered her something," he murmured, rubbing the unblemished side of his forehead. "Everyone has their price, I suppose." His mouth twisted as if he'd eaten something rotten. As if the words didn't sit right in his tongue.

"Maybe they forced it out of her," she offered. "Do you have any clue who might want to kill you?"

"That's a looooong list."

"Fine, different approach. The bounty hunter said a king was dead. What does that mean?"

Bast scoffed and lowered his head. "Easy. My father has passed."

Mera gasped. "What?"

"He died, and someone wants me to do the same," he spoke slowly, as if she was daft. "Which is odd. I'm the last in line for the throne, and besides, I was disowned a long time ago."

"What about the first in line?" Mera asked, shocked at Bast's reaction—or lack thereof. "Aren't they in danger? Shouldn't we contact the night fae jurisdiction?"

"Leon?" He chortled. "I'd know if he wasn't okay, trust me. Also, we do have a precinct, but it's been empty for decades."

This was getting weirder by the second. "You're on an island. Tagrad should have some representation there."

"It does. The Night King works as a sort of deputy, which means the court's guards are effectively Tagradian police." He shrugged. "Besides, if there's a problem, Tir Na Nog officers liaise with local forces by flying there or taking a boat. The waters are protected anyway, and the island isn't that far."

So, night fae had carte blanche to do whatever they wanted in their territory. Either the Tagradian government was really stupid, or they really trusted them.

Mera rubbed the bridge of her nose, feeling an oncoming headache. "Okay, fine, it doesn't matter. But Bast, we *have* to take this to Captain Asherath."

He stood up and went to one of the chairs on the dining table, where he'd dropped his sleeping clothes in the morning. Removing his pants, Bast showcased black boxers that fit him stupidly well.

Mera looked away, but heard him chuckling in the background.

"Stop pretending to be such a prude, kitten. We technically had sex."

She blushed furiously. "It was just a dream!"

"Keep telling yourself that," he mocked. "You can look now."

Even with a black T-shirt and shorts, Bast was outstanding. It didn't seem fair to her that one single male could look this... perfect.

'Arousing is the right word,' her siren whispered.

Shooting up to her feet, Mera slammed both hands on her waist. "Look, whoever is out for you clearly won't drop the bone until you're dead. Ignoring the problem won't solve anything."

"I know." He stepped closer and laid a warm, heavy hand on her shoulder. "I'll deal with it, I promise. But we have a murder to solve first, hopefully before whoever hired that assassin realizes he's dead."

She nodded, relaxing under his touch, but wondered if she should tell him what was on her mind. "Bast, your father died. It's okay to mourn him."

Even Mera had mourned Queen Ariella in her own way. She'd mourned the opportunities they'd missed, the moments they would never share. Most of all, she mourned for the mother she never had.

"I'm fine." He threw himself on the sofa and closed his eyes. "Good night."

"Will you please inform Captain Asherath tomorrow? You don't need to tell him you killed a defenseless faerie, but he should be informed that your life is in danger." She tapped her temple. "Why not contact him right now with that magic line you both share?"

"He has a life and we're off work." He inhaled deeply. "I suppose we can stop by the precinct tomorrow, before we pay a visit to Zev Ferris' poker buddies. Would that make you stop nagging me?"

"It would." She headed to her room, feeling as if Bast was the siren who dragged her under.

He left a body trail in his wake, and Mera covered for him. Granted, it had been a matter of survival, literally, and not at all different from what she'd done to her mother. Still, it didn't sit right in her throat.

Maybe Mera could bring him back to the surface. Maybe she could save him from himself.

Stopping by the bedroom door, she turned around. "Bast, I know you've never had a proper partner before, so you don't know what to expect. But you're not alone in this, okay?"

A dashing grin tilted his lips, but his eyes remained closed. "Stop smothering me, partner."

The next morning, Bast landed them on the rooftop of his precinct.

Mera had tied her hair in a low braid before they'd soared into the sky, that way, her hairdo kept neatly in place, even after Bast took them on a large loop moments before landing.

"We should've taken this entrance when we first came in," she admitted, exhilaration still lingering in her veins.

"I didn't think you'd enjoy flying so much." He stepped closer and placed a hand on the curve of her waist, but removed it quickly when a faerie wearing a navy suit and a sequoia shirt passed by them.

He nodded at Bast before his purple wings spread wide, and then off he went into the sky. Mera couldn't say if she was angry or grateful for the interruption.

Bast showed her the entrance. "Let's get this over with so we can continue our investigation, shall we?"

They went down the stairs, and knocked on the captain's door.

A faerie with pinkish hair and canary skin welcomed them. He was shorter than Bast and wore a white captain's uniform. His cheeks glittered as if they'd been dusted with golden powder.

"Detective Dhay," he greeted in a monotone voice. "I was hoping you'd come by. I'm your new Captain, Solomon Cane." He offered him his hand.

Bast's jaw hung open. "Where's Captain Asherath?"

"He took a leave of absence."

"Leave of absence, my ass." Bast's fists closed, and he stepped forward. "Where's my captain, *baku*?"

"I'll forget you've insulted your superior." Solomon held both hands behind his back, arching a pink eyebrow. "Apparently, your Captain had a knack for mishandling evidence. Everyone knows the Tir Na Nog precinct can bend the rules to get things done, but mishandling evidence is not something the government of Tagrad can overlook."

"The phone." Bast stepped back. "Where's Redford?"

Solomon gave him a pleased grin that reminded Mera of a hyena. "Under investigation. You mishandled evidence, Detective. So did your captain. However, the Summer King's family was kind enough to forgive your mishap. You should be grateful. Captain Asherath wasn't so lucky, considering his feud with the Autumn Court."

"You fucking bastard," Mera muttered, disgust reeling through her.

With a huff, Solomon ignored her, certainly deeming a human not worth the bother.

"Why not punish me?" Bast asked, confusion in his tone. "I'm the one who made the mistake, not Fallon or Redford."

"Politics, I suppose." Solomon shrugged nonchalantly. "By the way, the faerie who killed Zev Ferris confessed."

No. Way.

"What did you just say?" Mera asked, hoping she'd misheard him.

"The Summer King wronged the culprit in a game of cards. What a dull reason for such an elaborate murder, don't you think? He'll spend the rest of his life without seeing the light of day, which is a fate worse than death for a Summer faerie." He patted Bast's shoulder. "Good job, Detective. Please arrange for the return of your human partner to Clifftown, where she belongs."

"Where I *belong*?" Mera stepped forward, ready to teach this dickwart the lesson of a lifetime. "Who do you think you are, you giant fuc—"

Bast grabbed her wrist and shook his head. The worry in his eyes silenced Mera.

To enforce the law in Tir Na Nog, one had to bend it a little. Every decent fae out there did it, as long as the result was a win for Tagrad. The light courts had been counting on that, waiting for the perfect moment to strike.

"We are happy the case is solved," Bast assured with a strain in his neck. "*Captain*."

"Good. You've been working tirelessly for the past years." Solomon tapped his arm. "Why don't you accompany Detective Maurea back to her precinct, and then take some time off? You deserve it, officer Dhay."

A certain calm took over Bast. His shoulders dropped and he gave Solomon the fakest of grins. "Of course. Thank you, Captain."

Taking Mera's hand, he pulled her out of the precinct, never bothering to look back. Mera did, though, and saw Solomon waving at them with a cruel smirk.

This was wrong. So very wrong.

She glanced down at her hand in Bast's, their fingers intertwined. A blush rose to her cheeks, even if unwarranted.

Leading her into the street, he let go of her hand, and spun around. A mix of bewilderment and desperation marred his face. "This is bad."

Mera glanced back at the precinct's glass building, the

one place that represented Hollowcliff and Tagrad in this cursed borough.

The last stand.

It had been taken down from the inside.

Yeah.

They had a huge fucking problem.

CHAPTER 17

Bᴀꜱᴛ ꜱᴀᴛ ᴏɴ ᴛʜᴇ ꜱᴏꜰᴀ, hunched over his knees. He hid his face behind his palms, and if Mera didn't know better, she would say the Night Prince-slash-detective might be praying.

"It was bound to happen," he said, his voice muffled behind his hands, "just not so soon. And not like this."

She dropped on the padded cushion beside him, not knowing what to say or do. "What if we tell the government?"

It was a stupid idea. She realized it the moment she said it aloud. Solomon had been sanctioned through the proper channels. He'd provided evidence against Captain Asherath, and as far as the papers went, he'd done right by Tagradian law.

Evidence was sacred. Everyone knew that.

Asherath and Bast had ignored this simple rule, because they feared the corruption in the Tir Na Nog precinct⬜clearly with reason.

A mistake, granted. With giant consequences.

Not that the government was wrong—if Mera messed with evidence back in Clifftown, she would lose her badge, and maybe even go to prison. Yes, tampering with evidence in the human borough was bad, but doing it in Tir Na Nog? It might be the only way to catch the bad guys.

She understood that now.

Bast leaned back on the sofa, his eyes closed. He stayed in silence for a while. His strong Adam's apple bobbed up and down every so often, and her siren wanted to lick it.

He seemed incredibly peaceful, even though he must have been writhing inside.

'Smell the curve of his neck,' the horny bastard inside Mera whispered.

"Like what you see, kitten?" he asked, his eyes still closed.

She crossed her arms and leaned back on the couch, glad that he couldn't see her blushing.

"Oh, wow, he's awake." Softly, she kicked his left shin. "What are you doing?"

"Talking to Captain Asherath. He's safe." He opened his eyes, but a concerned frown marred his forehead. "He's with Stella."

"He is?"

"We arranged for this a while ago." Bast must've noticed the question on her face. "Fallon always knew our safety bubble was fragile, but we were getting somewhere, kitten. We were this close..." He grunted what sounded like *malachais* under his breath, and sitting up abruptly, his palm slammed on the coffee table. "That's how those assholes got to him. By making him look dirty. Fallon is the most trust-worthy fae in the entire borough!"

"It stinks of a political maneuver."

"That's because it is." His lips curled in the way of a lion about to prowl. "The Autumn Court wanted his head for a long time. And I delivered it on a platter to them."

"You can't blame yourself for this." She laid a gentle hand on his shoulder. "If we had followed procedure, we wouldn't have gotten the phone in the first place. You said it yourself, to fight for justice in Tir Na Nog, we can't play by the rules."

His breathing slowly steadied, his anger not gone, merely contained.

"You're right," he conceded. "The captain is pissed. He wants to go to Clifftown with proof of corruption and ill intent." Bast ran a hand over his face. "He says he has enough to squeeze Solomon and get to whoever supported this coup. Only problem is, the courts are after Fallon. And I doubt they'll make an arrest if they find him."

Yeah, she doubted that too. "Is there any way we can help?"

Bast clicked his tongue. "Solomon will be keeping an eye on us. We could lead him straight to Fallon, *and* my sister."

A definite no, then.

"He's safe with Stella, for the time being," Bast assured. "We aren't registered as siblings since she's a halfling. Father never acknowledged her."

"And most Sidhe are snobbish bastards who tend to ignore halflings," Mera added. "Which makes her place a perfect hideout."

Her partner winked at her. "You're not just for looks, kitten."

She hated herself for blushing.

"Bast, this wouldn't have happened if we hadn't come close to something serious. There's incriminating evidence on that phone, I can feel it. Something the light courts want silenced, and it has to do with the murders. It's all connected."

He nodded. "Whoever is behind Zev Ferris and Sara Hyland's murders got Solomon his new job."

She clapped her hands and stood, reeling in the adrenaline of the hunt. "Okay, here's what we know so far: Sara Hyland was pregnant with a magical child, but it wasn't Zev's. She was drowned after someone stupefied her right here in Tir Na Nog."

"Zev's last message said he'd protect her. Maybe that's why she came."

"Right. Do you think she needed protection from the baby's father? Maybe he belonged to one of the light courts."

"Seems likely. Sara Hyland was a drug dealer. She walked with a bad crowd, so maybe that's how she met her abusive baby daddy. But it also led her to Zev." He lifted a finger. "Wait." A smile caressed his lips. "Stella found someone to winnow her and Captain Asherath to Clifftown."

"She's talking to you?"

"Of course she is." He sounded insulted. "You think I'd have a channel to Fallon but not to my own sister?" Before Mera could reply he waved a hand at her. "I also used to have it with my brother Leon, but it's grown weaker. Now, I would only sense him if our bond vanished."

Meaning when one of them died.

No wonder Bast was so sure his brother was safe.

"Hey!" He frowned and stared past Mera, into an empty space. For a moment, she wondered if he had lost his mind.

"Stella, tell him to stop looking at you like that." Silence ensued, then, "Stella, I swear…" Bast paused as if listening to her. "But you're my sis—" He cursed under his breath.

Mera guessed Stella had disconnected.

"Everything okay?"

"Fucking splendid," he grunted, running a hand through his hair, and studying his own feet. "I keep wondering why Sara had the name Poseidon in her notebook."

Mera shrugged and feigned nonchalance. "Coincidence? Come on, Bast, we've gone over this. Mermaids can't enter the forbidden zone."

His forehead wrinkled. "You mean *protection* zone?"

Falling into an endless pit within herself, she blinked. "Yes. Protection zone. That's what I meant." Mera cleared her throat. "Mermaids can't enter Tagradian sea or land, and live to tell the tale. Sara would have to swim for at least two hours to even meet one."

Humans couldn't swim as fast as sirens, so it would've taken Sara hours to cover the distance Mera could do in a minute.

"Also," she added, "how could a mermaid bring her body back to shore without dying in the process?"

"It does sound impossible," Bast muttered, thoughts blasting behind his eyes.

She let out a discrete, relieved breath. Thankfully, her phone rang at that precise moment.

It was Jules.

A knot formed in her gut, but Mera couldn't tell why.

"Hey," he greeted from the other side. "The Cap told me you guys caught the culprit and that you're coming back on Thursday?"

"Yeah," she lied, knowing better than to tell him the truth, at least for the time being. She'd already made him accessory to tampering of evidence; she couldn't make him accessory to whatever she and Bast were about to do.

"Finally." There was a smile in his voice. "Do you need what we found on the phone?"

"You found something?"

"Jim from IT picked up a deleted sound file. We were able to recover it from the cloud server, but it doesn't shed any light to the case."

She sat back on the sofa and pressed a button on her phone. "Jules, you're on speaker."

"Hey, assface," Julian said from the other side.

Bast grinned ferociously. "Dickwart."

Damn it, she'd taught him that word.

"Mera and I have been having so much fun," Bast teased. "Just the other day, we had mind-blowing sex and—"

She slapped his arm so hard that Julian might've heard it.

"Ouch!" He rubbed the spot, but the grin on his face told her she should've hit him way harder.

"Mera, what the…" Julian stopped himself. "Nevermind."

"He's just being a nasty fae. We didn't have sex." Mera's face burned so hot it might have melted. "Hit me with what you found, Jules."

He was awfully silent for a moment, his anger cutting for miles and burning through the speaker.

"Sending it right away," he finally spoke, his tone bitterly cold.

Fuck… Mera would have to deal with that later.

The wi-fi reception in Tir Na Nog was utter crap, but eventually she received the file. "All right, got it. I'll call you back."

The recording started with the rushed breaths of someone on the run. Finally, a strong voice blared through the speaker.

"My name is Zev Ferris, and I don't trust the Tir Na Nog precinct to see this through. We, the light courts, have created a monster that even Captain Asherath can't control." He took a deep breath. "Fallon, if you ever hear this, I'm sorry. I'm sorry for making your life harder, for not standing up to August when he exiled you from Autumn. I know there's little you can do to help me right now, and that this is partially my fault. I'm sorry for that, too. I'll leave my phone here, in Clifftown. They'll get to the bottom of this."

Mera pressed pause as she and Bast stared at each other. For a moment, she forgot how to breathe, but by the shock on Bast's face, so had he.

"This might be the motherload, kitten," he whispered, his eyes glinting with anticipation.

She pressed play.

"Someone is after my friend Sara Hyland. I believe it's the father of her child. I took her to Tir Na Nog under my protection, but he must have found her and winnowed her back to Clifftown. I'm taking Sara away from Tagrad as soon as I locate her. To whomever listens to this: you must stop him. Only then will Sara be safe."

Mera assumed he'd halted, since it sounded like he was catching his breath.

"I love her," he stated simply.

A fact. A vow.

"You should know why I'm doing this," he continued. "Why the king of the Summer Court is willing to risk everything for a human who isn't carrying his own offspring."

A car drove nearby and honked. Zev probably had no clue how to cross a street in Clifftown.

More hushed breaths followed, then a guy yelled in the distance, "Hey, watch where you goin', asshole!"

"The location sorcery on my phone has taken me to Sara's building," Zev panted. Mera caught the sound of keys jingling in the background. "Find the mad seer. She speaks in riddles but listen carefully. If you're worthy, she'll give you what you need." The click of a front door opening echoed. "I must make sure Sara is safe. May your Gods and mine have mercy on us both."

End of the recording.

Holy. Fucking. Shit.

Mera stared at a befuddled Bast, still not believing what they'd heard.

"How can we find this mad seer?" she asked.

"Lucky for us, she lives in Tir Na Nog," Bast said, deep in

thought. "My precinct might not excel when it comes to technology, but they'll find that recording soon enough, kitten."

She nodded. "We need to hurry."

CHAPTER 18

Somewhere in the past...

MERA FLOATED close to the ocean's sandy bottom, dread gnawing at her chest. A line of waterbreakers wearing fighting corals stood ahead in the distance.

Please don't...

Battle cries suddenly erupted from their throats, their furious screams sending ripples across the water. They boosted forward and flung themselves into the forbidden zone.

"Mother, tell them to stop," Mera begged, her entire body shivering even though she couldn't feel cold—not unless she swam into the trenches, where there was no light, no life, nothing but darkness.

"No," the queen replied, her tone colder than what the deepest part of the trenches must have felt like. "Their sacrifice is their duty."

Her silver crown with sapphire beads matched her blue

and green war corals, but not her skirt. The queen had once found a skeleton wearing a cape inside an ancient shipwreck —at least Professor Currenter had said the thing was called a cape. Since then, she wrapped it around her waist and used it in every big event in Atlantea.

The cape—now technically a skirt according to the professor—flowed lazily behind her, following the slow rhythm of the currents. Its algae-green color had nearly faded; the fabric tattered on the edges.

Mera once dared ask why Mother loved it so much.

"It comes from a dead landrider." The queen had turned to her and bit into the head of a small fish, chewing the skin and bone with her sharp teeth. *"I like it, just because."*

A thumping sound coming from behind jolted Mera from her memories.

She turned back to see hundreds of Atlanteans placing limestone blocks atop each other. Carriages led by giant seahorses took the heavy loads to the site, dropping them near a system of levers and ropes that helped raise the blocks and place them in neat stacks.

A metallic drone led one of the carts. The thing was shaped like a stingray and it moved with the same easy flow, its glowing blue eyes shining without a soul within.

Her mother loved experimenting with what landriders called technology. It was why Atlantea had strong structures able to withstand wild currents, weapons that could cut through the hardest of stones, corals that cast light into the darkness, and now these test vehicles Mother would be implementing soon.

Technology had also given them the scaled bodysuits that worked as a second skin. They'd been annoying at first, but Mera was used to her own deep green suit by now.

The workers, much like Mera, avoided looking at the carnage ahead, though they could hear the screams.

Everyone could.

Mother's atrium would be finished soon. It faced that particular patch of the forbidden zone, which she said was the weakest area of the invisible wall.

"Watch," the queen ordered.

Mera turned toward the horrors ahead, knowing the heavy price of disobeying her.

As soon as the soldiers pierced into the forbidden zone, a purple pulse swam through the barrier, disappearing as fast as it came. Instantly, purple and dark rust began consuming the soldiers' bodies.

It was a slow process, but not slow enough to let them go far.

Their screams were no longer filled with bravery and resilience, but with terror and pain. Their horrid shrieks cut through the water and Mera's flesh, piercing deep into her bones, settling into her essence forever.

Some soldiers dared swim back, but the rust ate at them before they could reach safety. Then they had no more throats to scream, no more skin and bone. The rust ate it all away. Their armors collapsed onto the sandy ocean floor as their ashes puffed into sluggish clouds.

Queen Ariella watched, her clear green eyes narrowed.

"Mother, please," Mera croaked. "They are our people."

"Yes, they are." She held her silver triton high and the next batch of soldiers boosted forward, their brave screams an exact copy of their predecessors. "That's why they sacrifice."

Mera looked away, but her mother leaned down and grabbed her chin with long, piercing nails that dug into her skin. Mera could smell droplets of her own blood in the water.

The queen forced her head towards the massacre. "You will watch, weakling," she hissed, poison and hatred in her tone. "You'll watch it, and honor their sacrifice. It's the least those brave souls deserve."

She eyed her own daughter with disgust, but Mera was used to it by now. On a good day, that was how Mother regarded her—with contempt and disappointment. On a bad day...

Mera didn't want to remember those. Still, she couldn't bear the sight of so many deaths, not anymore.

"This is how you get to them, *Mother*," she blurted, knowing common sense had abandoned her altogether. "You speak of honor and sacrifice, and yet you stay here and watch while others die for your ambition."

Mother's fingers dug harder into her skin, drawing more blood, and Mera never felt so small, so weak.

So incredibly powerless.

The queen squeezed harder, until Mera thought her jaw might grind into dust. "Does defying me bring you joy?"

No. Nothing did. And Mera was tired.

Three years ago, she'd promised Professor Currenter she wouldn't defy her mother.

She couldn't keep that promise anymore.

Not today.

"You're a fraud," she managed through clenched teeth.

Queen Ariella's green eyes widened, the glassy beads reflecting the ocean around them, and the sheer fear in Mera's face. The beating of a lifetime would be waiting for Mera back home, inside the beautiful façade of their silver palace.

"Do you hate me, daughter?" she asked with genuine curiosity, never letting go of Mera's jaw.

Yes.

Mera didn't understand why she couldn't say it out loud. Maybe she feared the beating that would follow. Maybe she was terrified she didn't actually hate her mother.

Maybe both.

"You're weak and unworthy of my throne," Queen Ariella snapped upon her silence. "Yet, you are your father's daughter, and my hands are tied."

"Liar," Mera spat. "I'm your only remaining heir. That's why you don't kill me. It has nothing to do with who my supposed father is."

Her mother chortled as she released her. Mera drew in a big breath through the gills behind her temples and near her ribcage, glad that the ocean took away her tears.

"Wrong. I can always make more of you. I always have, in fact," the queen said with amusement. "All I need is to take one of the servants into my bedroom, and soon enough, I could give you a brother or sister."

Mera frowned, not knowing how taking a servant into her chambers could give her mother an offspring, but she made a note to ask Professor Currenter later.

"Maybe they would be weak like you," the queen continued. "Maybe they would be strong and challenge me, like many of your dead siblings. It's always a gamble." She narrowed her eyes at Mera. "Yet, you intrigue me in your weakness, daughter, for it is also your strength. I want to see how far you'll go before I chop off your head."

Mera had never felt so alone, so insignificant. Anger swam through her, cold and sharp.

Merciless.

"Did you tell Atlantea my brothers and sisters were children of Poseidon, too?"

"Perhaps I did." A cruel smirk hooked up on the left side of her cheek. "You're too smart for your own good, weakling. Now, watch."

Mera turned to see empty war corals falling to the ocean floor, cutting through clouds of ashes. Once again, her mother raised her triton, lowering it, and the third batch of merfolk went screaming to their deaths.

"Landrider magic has limits," the queen explained with a shrug. "Our magic, however, is taken from the water, and water is all around us. It's also everywhere on the surface. This is why most landriders, magical or not, perish when faced with the macabre."

Mera frowned as she watched the soldiers crumble into dust. "You're trying to see what it takes to break the barrier."

Professor Currenter had once said that facing Queen Ariella was like staring at an untamed great white shark. He was right, of course, and yet, for the first time in her life, Mera spotted pride behind her mother's cruel, lifeless eyes.

"You take after me, daughter." She smirked. "Much as you hate it."

Bile swirled in Mera's gut, a bitter taste that went up to her mouth.

"Land fae are also made of magic," she countered quietly. "Professor Currenter said we used to be known as sea fae once. It's land fae magic in that barrier, Mother."

"We are nothing like them," the queen spat. "And their magic is weak. You'll see."

Atlanteans kept shooting themselves into their deaths. Mera's shock and anger had slowly vanished, replaced by a deep numbness. She might as well be watching baby crabs killing themselves for no reason.

Mera hated it; hated the waterbreaker she was becoming.

Mother's masterpiece.

The fourth batch was getting ready. They didn't carry the same foolish bravery as their brothers and sisters who'd perished, and still, they would fling themselves into the forbidden zone without second thought.

For honor. For Atlantea.

For their queen.

"Is their blood worth your experiment?" Mera pointed toward the forbidden zone. "What if it takes all of us to break it?"

"Unlikely." Her mother raised her shoulders, reddish-brown hair flowing sluggishly around her. "It will break before then. As I've said, fae or not, landrider magic is weak."

"You're wrong," she muttered. "We'll all be dead before the barrier shatters. Perhaps you'll be happy when you're the last waterbreaker left in the sea."

The queen glared down at Mera, and her nostrils flared.

Ariella Wavestorm had tried to end Mera's life before—and rather often—but this time she would truly do it.

"They are sacrificing themselves for their queen." Her mother slapped her face with her free hand, then clawed at Mera's chest, drawing blood. "They understand this is how we bring our vengeance upon the surface people."

The fleshy rips on her skin stung against the ocean's salt. Mera held the cry and the tears that pushed out as she put a hand over the wound, trying to stop the bleeding, but her hand wasn't big enough to cover the cuts.

She was just a merling who hadn't even reached her blooming years. And yet, she'd already learned how to mask pain.

Yes, Mera was young, but she felt old and withered.

The queen raised her chin and her arm, sending the final batch into the forbidden zone. "Sometimes I wonder if you truly came out of me."

Mera hated that the words hurt. She didn't want to be like her mother, and if that meant she was weak and pathetic, then great.

The rejection still stung, though.

"Landriders banished us centuries ago," Mera pushed, hoping common sense would win over her mother's bloodthirst. "We're happy here, and Atlantea is thriving under your rule. Why waste lives trying to conquer the surface?"

The queen turned to her at once, and Mera jerked back, her heart beating madly in her chest. Her wounds bled faster.

"Because it all belongs to *us*!" She kept swimming forward while Mera swam back. "Water and land, they're both Poseidon's gift to *us*, not them! The surface is ours, and we must reclaim it!" Madness flooded her mother's beady green eyes, the same eyes Mera had inherited. The queen slapped her left cheek so violently, Mera's skin and bone thumped. "Do not question me again, or I swear to you, it will be the last thing you do."

"But—"

"Go away, merling." She waved her hand, dismissing her. "Go away, before I end you."

And she would. She truly would.

Mera had lost count of the times her mother had beaten her to the edge of unconsciousness, only to be stopped by the mercy of one of her advisors.

Like Professor Currenter.

"You shouldn't speak against your mother, princess," he said later that day, as he rubbed a concoction of mud and algae over the wounds. "She wants war, and war is what she'll have."

"She's killing us." Mera winced as the concoction burned against the cuts.

Blue wisps of light flowed from the professor's hands into her bruises, numbing the pain. "Those soldiers volunteered for the task." He finished the patch and wrapped a strip of algae around Mera's chest. "There you go. Give it half a day and you'll be as good as new, little fry."

Mera shook her head, glancing out the round window of

Professor Currenter's cave. "What happens when she runs out of soldiers?"

"Your mother is smart." He put a heavy hand on her shoulder. "The real question is, what happens when she runs out of *expendable* soldiers?"

"I pray to Poseidon that day never comes."

Professor Currenter smiled sadly. "There's not enough prayer in the seven seas to quench the queen's thirst for blood, my dear princess."

~

The atrium was finished in record time.

Limestone pews piled atop each other, forming a half circle that faced the ocean ahead. The invisible entrance to the forbidden zone.

The pews were packed with merfolk, who watched with either dread or anticipation. Mera couldn't tell how many supported her mother's actions, and how many disapproved of them, but an awfully great number considered the mass killings a necessary evil to progress.

Mera despised them the most; those Atlanteans who raved for the queen, for the progress she brought to the sea, but ignored the price.

Queen Ariella swam forward and out of her seat, floating before the audience. Down below, soldiers pressed a crowd of waterbreakers into a tight circle.

"Merfolk of Atlantea," the queen's voice echoed throughout the space, boosted by the small device attached to the corner of her mouth. "We are here today to honor the sacrifice of our brothers and sisters!"

The soldiers forced the crowd in the circle forward, forming a line headed to the forbidden zone. A whirlpool followed the queue, thrashing above the prisoners' heads and preventing them from escaping.

Waterbending was a basic skill for every waterbreaker, but the soldiers' abilities clearly outweighed those of the civilians about to meet their end.

The group pushed back against the soldiers, but these were fishermen and builders, teachers and weavers with no experience in battle.

Queen Ariella raised her silver triton and everyone silenced. Even the doomed stopped fighting.

"May Poseidon find you on the day of Regneerik, brothers and sisters. May he call you to his side for your bravery!" She lowered the triton.

Belinda Tiderider's mother headed the line. Mera knew her from the times she had lunch at her friend's home, or the nights they'd spent studying for tests.

Salina was as beautiful as her daughter. They shared the same sandy blond hair and pinkish hue to their hides, the same bright purple irises.

Belinda's mother had always been kind to Mera. This was what she envied the most about Belinda; not her developed bosom, not the attention she got from every young male in school, but the fact she had a caring, loving mother who cheered for her at school sport events, who supported her through everything she did. A mother who hugged her daughter and told her she loved her.

A bitter taste flooded Mera's mouth, and she searched frantically for her best friend, hoping, praying she wasn't in the doomed crowd with Salina.

Luckily, she wasn't. She did, however, sit on one of the pews below, forced to watch.

Belinda was trembling. She grasped the rails of the pews so hard that tiny cracks spread on the limestone underneath her fingertips.

Mera's heart beat in her temples as she saw Salina step into the forbidden zone.

Instead of trying to swim away or put up any fight, she turned around and faced the soldiers. She then faced the queen herself, in one last act of defiance.

Mera wondered why those Atlanteans had been chosen. Were they a nuisance to her mother? Did they belong to the weakened resistance that defied Ariella's rule?

Salina Tiderider kept staring at her mother as purple and black rust began eating away at her skin, her glare calling Ariella the forbidden name whispered in the streets of Atlantea.

Mad Queen.

She did not scream, even as the rust ate away her arms and legs. She merely stared.

This time at Mera.

And in that bitter stare, Mera saw herself turning into Mother. She saw a murderer and a monster, stopping at nothing to get the bloodbath her predecessor craved. A mad sovereign, aching for the approval her mother would never give.

After all, the queen tried to shape Mera to her image. It was why she made her watch as her own people died, made her suffer until all the fight in her subdued.

As the rust ate away Salina's fierce, judging eyes, Mera understood. It had always been about survival. Either hers or Mother's.

The thought terrified her.

Mera was just a merling. She wasn't strong or fast and she wasn't ready to die—but neither were those Atlanteans down below.

The atrium went silent like the dead. Silent like Salina Tiderider. Even Belinda held back the sounds of her grief, her hands clasped over her mouth as her shoulders shook.

The silence settled over Mera like a cape, smothering her fear, leaving no room in her mind for anything but cold determination.

She swam forward as the queen ordered the next civilian's doom.

"What are you doing, weakling?" Mother snapped at her with gritted teeth. "Go back to your seat."

"I defy you," she spoke quietly. "In the name of Poseidon, god of the seas, I defy you."

"You use your father's name in vain." That mad, furious glare that turned an otherwise pretty waterbreaker into a monster, took over her mother's face.

"He's not my father," she spat. "And you're a liar."

If Poseidon was truly her father, he would've taken Mera from this miserable life a long time ago.

In one quick move, the queen grabbed the rusted sword attached to her war corals, pressing it against Mera's throat. "Defy me again, merling," she leaned closer, "and you will not live another day."

"I challenge you!" Mera screamed, her voice captured by the device on Mother's mouth, booming so loudly that not just the audience and the soldiers, but all of Atlantea must've heard her.

Shocked gasps rang from everywhere around them.

As mad as her mother had become, she knew the rules. The queen might be able to enforce much of her will, such as ordering her own people to a senseless death, but when one of her own bloodline challenged her, she was obligated to accept. If she killed Mera right now, defenseless and without a chance to fight, then Atlanteans were bound to do the same to her. Mera guessed many in this atrium needed the excuse.

Belinda especially.

Yes, the law protected Mera. A royal challenge demanded a battle, but she hoped she'd angered the queen enough for her to make a move. If Mother killed Mera right now, she'd give Atlanteans a reason to tear her apart.

Let Mera's death serve a purpose.

The crowd around them stood still and deadly silent, certainly expecting Mera's end.

She was ready.

"I volunteer!" Professor Currenter swam forward, despair in his eyes, his hands balled into fists. "I volunteer to take the princess' place!"

Mera skipped a breath as panic took over. He was the only good thing in her life. If he died in her place... Mera couldn't fathom what she would do.

Thankfully, her mother was swift. "Denied. The blood challenge shall not be extended."

"She's just a youngling, my queen," the professor begged. "Have mercy!"

Ariella clicked her tongue, watching him with disgust. "So soft... Smart, valuable," she said as if justifying his existence, "but so terribly soft."

She turned to Mera. "The challenge is accepted."

The queen removed the device from the corner of her mouth and lowered her sword. "You should've flung yourself into that barrier, weakling," she whispered. "You would have been more useful to me."

CHAPTER 19

Still in the past...

PROFESSOR CURRENTER FIXED the back straps of Mera's armor.

Her battle clothes were made of shark leather, with blue and white corals sewn to it that protected her chest, stomach, waist, and knees. Underneath, she wore a navy bodysuit, with scales that glinted against the light from the neon corals peppering the professor's cave.

Mera watched herself in the standing mirror, which leaned on the wall close to the round window. The professor had fixed her hair in a high braid, the way most female soldiers wore it.

The mirror was reminiscent of his time on the surface, for he'd been a youngling when the war broke, over one thousand years ago. Nowadays, plenty of Atlantean households had mirrors. It was easy to forge them by channeling the heat of the lava pits into refined sand—thanks to her mother's *technology*.

The dark stone walls of the professor's place were uneven and unpolished, a nod to how Atlanteans used to live back in the day.

Most households now had smooth curved walls of the brightest colors, and many held special advancements to help with everyday tasks, such as the repurposed rainbow-neon corals with intensified glow which Mother named *lamps*.

Funny that the apparatus resembled the broken lamps found in shipwrecks.

The queen loved her precious *technology*, but in the end, it was nothing more than a copy from the world above. A yearning for things no merfolk could have.

Through the window, Mera observed the neon town ahead, its lights dimmed by faint sunlight coming from the surface. The light hit a silver spot that glinted in the distance.

Atlantea's castle. Beautiful on the outside, wretched within.

Mera hated the gloomy and empty stone corridors, the silent servants, her endless beatings and echoing screams.

It would all end today.

The castle might be a beacon of the modernizing era the mad queen pushed forward, the apex of her rule, which had given her many supporters, but those halls were as rotten and ugly as Ariella herself.

Professor Currenter tugged the straps tighter, and Mera turned back to the mirror. She looked small and scrawny against her armor.

Most Atlanteans only joined the military after their coming of age. The armors available hadn't been made to protect a child, and even though Professor Currenter had adjusted as much as he could, her battle wear was still enormous. And heavy.

Moving would be a problem, not that being fast could save her anyway.

Nothing could.

"You can't win by using strength," the professor advised as he clipped the straps, making it hard for Mera to breathe. Today he wore yellow fighting corals over his black scaled clothing, his white hair trapped in a tight bun.

In putting on his own battle wear, he honored her.

After all, this was Mera's funeral.

"Use the water," he added quietly, avoiding eye contact. "Fight like we've practiced so many times. And use the macabre. I know I told you to control it, but let it consume you, just this once."

Had he lost his mind?

"Using the macabre in a royal challenge is forbidden," she reminded him. "The punishment is death."

"We'll cross that valley when we get to it," he assured. "First, you must survive. No matter what, Mera."

Resignedly, she shook her head. "Mother is stronger in every way. I'm not leaving that arena alive."

He didn't deny it.

"The queen calls you daughter of Poseidon," he stated, adjusting the back of her armor, pulling and knotting the straps, trying to adapt it to her frail body as much as he could. "The gods may not be real, but I've come to think she calls you that because she favors you."

Mera chortled, but the professor didn't seem amused.

"I hope that in her madness, in thinking you're the daughter of a god, she might show you mercy," he added quietly.

"You know my mother. Being merciful isn't one of her qualities."

Mera's life was pure torture, thanks to queen Ariella. Not only that, but Mother was now slaughtering her own people, left and right. Yet, none of the grownups dared to go against her. None dared to say "Enough."

It wasn't fair that a merling had to do it.

Not that it mattered.

Mera had a terrible, agonizing existence. Unloved by her own mother, tortured and beaten through most of her days, she would finally find peace. Dying today was the only mercy the queen would grant her.

"If you win," the professor said, turning her around to face him. "Your uncle Barrimond will take the throne until you are of age. He's a good Atlantean, and not like your other uncles. He's strong enough to lead and keep them in place."

Uncle Barrimond had protected Mera from a beating once, standing between her and the queen. He would sneak sweets to Mera when her mother wasn't paying attention, and he also told her stories of brave warriors who fought for Atlantea and Poseidon.

"With pride and honor, they fought for glory," he used to say.

"Your uncle will give you the childhood you've always deserved, my little fry." The professor didn't actually believe this, Mera found fear and doubt in his face. His amber eyes glistened as he checked her armor, the water around them saltier than usual. "You are a flower born from a wasteland. The most precious—" His voice broke, and he lowered his head. "The most precious treasure in the seven seas. I am so proud of you."

Inhaling deeply, he clicked the last front straps and wiggled the armor, making sure it would hold in place. He then pulled Mera close in a tight hug, and put a hand over her head. They stayed that way for a long while, her little fingers digging against his back armor.

Mera would never meet her real father, but it didn't matter. Professor Currenter had done an extraordinary job in his place.

"Be strong, my brave princess." His breaths hitched. "You are too good for this world."

"Don't forget me, Professor." She held her tears. "I'll be meeting my brothers and sisters today."

Mera pulled away, grabbing the silver triton that rested against the stone wall on the right corner. It felt awfully heavy, but it was the smallest weapon they could find.

Time to face her end.

With pride. With honor...

Like those warriors in Uncle Barrimond's stories.

The arena was crowded. Rows upon rows circled around her, surrounding Mera in a dark tower that reached for the surface. A fiery gloom came from below, where a circling river of lava warmed the waters.

All it took was one steep dive and she'd melt into oblivion.

The atrium facing the forbidden zone had been an altar to sacrifice. This arena, with its ancient and uneven stone blocks, was an altar to battle, and Mera, merely a youngling, was here pretending to be a warrior.

Mother faced her as they both floated in the center of the space.

The queen wore starfish-red fighting corals with Orca leather straps. For the first time, Mera noticed how sharp the throngs of the royal triton were; how much bulkier the weapon seemed compared to hers.

The triton's spotless silver matched her mother's crown; the crown Mera would never get to wear. The queen had replaced its sapphire beads with rubies the color of blood, which mirrored her battle corals.

Mera held her triton so hard that her light gray knuckles went utterly white.

The crowd watched them, many with fear, many with excitement, some with horror, and others in disbelief.

The whole of Atlantea must be there today.

"You cannot kill me, weakling," Mother assured lowly. "Retract your challenge, and I might forgive you."

"You're not one to forgive," Mera countered, surprised at her own courage.

The queen smirked. "Your death will be meaningless."

"Perhaps, but I hope it will serve a purpose."

Fury raged inside Ariella's beady eyes. "And what purpose would that be?"

Gripping her triton harder, Mera pointed it at her. "Your end."

Mother cocked her head left, completely untouched by the threat. "In this world, the weak always die. There's no purpose in their passing, as you'll soon find out."

Mera swallowed dry, glancing at the thousands of water-breakers around her. A sour tang went down her throat as she asked herself why they didn't revolt. Why couldn't they put an end to the mad queen's reign?

Why did it have to be Mera floating there, without an army?

Without anyone.

"Mera Wavestorm!" someone yelled from the crowd, and her gaze flickered over the masses to find Belinda Tiderider.

Her friend gave her an approving nod, then closed her fist, thumping it against her chest. Most of her colleagues from school followed the gesture. So did Professor Currenter. Others in the audience joined them, though not many.

Not most.

Mera feared for her friends' lives. If the queen's wrath hit them... Her mother had already narrowed her eyes at them as if keeping track of their faces, but she couldn't remember them all.

She would remember Belinda, though, *and* Professor Currenter.

A horn sounded from above, a deep tune that reverberated into Mera's bones.

She bellowed a battle cry that birthed from deep within her soul, scraping the walls of her throat. Mera boosted forward, possessed by utter despair.

If her mother survived, the only two people she cared for would die.

The queen's face was full of surprise when her daughter nailed a punch on her left temple, sending her spinning away.

Mera didn't wait for her to recover; she couldn't afford to. She willed water currents forward, engulfing Ariella in a raging maelstrom.

"Silly games," her cruel voice boomed from inside the bubbling storm.

Mera felt her mother's magic pushing against hers, taking over the current. With one swing of her arm, the maelstrom vanished into thin water, revealing a warrior with a wicked grin, her bloodthirsty focus on her own child.

The queen flung her triton at her. Mera dodged it at the last minute, but one of the throngs ripped her shark-straps, releasing the coral over her stomach. The piece of armor plummeted toward the lava pit in a zig-zag.

"This ends today, weakling." Her mother's hands moved, and water rushed the triton back to her.

She jolted toward Mera, who managed to block the first attack with her frail weapon, the throngs of her triton jamming against her mother's.

Mera looped over the queen and got a free path to her

back. She kicked Ariella's spine, but Mother was faster and swiveled to the right. Grabbing Mera's ankle, she pulled her closer, then punched her unprotected stomach.

Mera bent over in pain as Ariella threw her triton upward. The queen joined both hands and smashed Mera's temple so hard, everything went dark for a second.

The arena spun around and Mera felt herself falling toward the fiery pit. She was still grasping her triton—the metal burned against her skin, so did the water.

The pain jolted Mera awake. Water boosted her up at her command, taking her higher until she was back in the battle space, facing her mother.

Mera could taste her own blood puffing around her and dispersing into the water.

"You should have burned, sweet Me-ra," Mother hissed, tasting the two syllables on her tongue, looking every bit the monster that she was.

"Some call you mad queen!" Mera yelled for everyone to hear. "They're right!"

Ariella snorted, but spotted the danger in her words. "Am I mad for bringing light to our city, laser guns to our army? For building homes that defy the harsh currents of the sea?" she asked the crowd. "Am I mad for wanting the future? For one day, taking us back to land?"

Cheers erupted from the crowd, but a nearly equal amount remained silent. Mera didn't know what to make of it.

"I don't care what you call me," the queen continued. "Yes, I ask much of you. But sacrifice yourselves to Poseidon, and he will bring you back on the day of Regneerik!"

"She's a liar!" Mera told them. "You will all die under her rule!"

"The sheer defiance!" The queen barked before boosting forward in rage.

Their tritons clanked loudly as she pushed Mera in a downwards spiral, forcing her to the bottom of the arena, where the lava pit waited for them. "Burn!" she bellowed, yellow and red flares highlighting the madness in her face.

Something inside Mera snapped.

Words could be a funny thing. She'd spoken them, she'd known their meaning, but it only hit her right then.

The queen had to die.

No matter what.

A strange force growled underneath Mera's skin, clawed at her veins. It spread from her core toward the crowd in a pulse, and suddenly she held all the lives of Atlantea in the palm of her hand.

She could feel their heartbeats. Their blood pumping. Their bellies rumbling.

Mera could feel *everything*.

She gaped at her own fingers, tightly wrapped around her triton as the heating water stung against her skin. She then turned to the queen, who smiled as they approached the lava.

Mera could feel her heartbeat, too.

The power that had spread across the arena sunk back into Mera, focusing on one Atlantean.

Her mother.

It pierced into the queen's magic as if it had been made of paper, and Ariella's pulse quickened.

She swam back at once, untangling her triton from Mera's, eyes widening as small veins bulged underneath her neck and cheeks.

"Impossible," she croaked.

The queen's magic tickled against Mera's macabre. She was trying to block her, but she failed miserably.

"I never mattered to you!" Mera shouted as she pushed her power forward, squeezing her mother's blood in and out of itself.

The queen yelped in pain. Ariella looked small, so very small. And Mera was big; no, she was enormous and unending.

Like the entire ocean.

"Your own people never mattered to you!" Mera faintly remarked the surge of power that pulsed from her, rippling toward the pews in the arena. Her fingers twisted, forcing the blood on her mother's hand.

The queen dropped the royal triton with a furious scream, and it sunk quickly into the lava below them.

She gaped at Mera, fear and anger fitting well inside her glassy green eyes. Ariella's macabre pushed against hers again, but Mera's power didn't budge.

"Mark my words, Mother," she vowed through gritted teeth. "I will make sure Poseidon never finds you, even if it's the last thing I do."

Stone rumbled around them, and merfolk screamed.

The power inside Mera had spread through the sea, pushing against the pews and the arena, the water thrashing wildly… *everywhere*.

She couldn't understand what was happening. A storm had taken over the space, rumbling toward the surface. The arena shook. Stone collapsed and Atlanteans shrieked in fear, but no one dared swim away, maybe because they didn't understand what was happening; maybe because the water outside the arena had become a flesh-ripping maelstrom.

Was Mera doing this?

Her mother took advantage of her distraction and freed herself from the macabre. She threw herself at Mera, howling her hatred away.

Out of instinct, Mera pushed her triton forward.

And into the queen.

The maelstrom vanished as Mera's power sunk back

inside her core. The screams waned. Mera couldn't hear the rumbling of stone, or the rushing of water anymore.

She glared at her impaled mother, and twisted the triton. Blood puffed in clouds around the wound, and it also came out from the corners of Mother's lips.

"You little—" the queen choked on her own blood. "You. From all who tried to end me… *you*," she spat, fury scorching her tone.

Mera's teeth gritted so hard she thought they might pulverize, but she didn't let go of the weapon.

The queen had to die.

She twisted it yet again, perfectly aware of the rivers of tears she gifted the ocean.

"I will never be like you, Mother," she croaked.

"No, weakling…" Staring at her, Ariella Wavestorm smiled. Her hand reached for Mera, caressing her cheek for the first and last time. "You're so much more."

Her body went limp on the triton.

A high-pitched tune took over Mera's ears, her vision blurring. Blood rushed through her veins and breathing became harder.

She'd killed her birth-giver.

The mad queen was no more.

Mera's hands brutally quivered, and the trembling swam through the triton, into the corpse, making her mother shake in an eerie dance.

A great sorrow filled her to the brim, soon becoming a dark boulder that crashed upon her without mercy. Mera hoped she would feel relief and joy, not this gut-gnawing anguish. Not this pain she couldn't understand or describe.

The arena was deadly silent. It looked off shape too—the tower bent slightly to the left.

The glares of Atlantea burned through her.

Professor Currenter dashed into the center and shook her awake from her shock. "You did it, little fry!"

A bulky waterbreaker with light-blue skin and hair yellow like the sun, floated above, in the middle of the arena. He nodded at her with a kind smile, then turned to the crowd. "Merfolk of Atlantea," Uncle Barrimond began, but Mera's attention drifted back to her triton and the dead body at its end.

Professor Currenter moved to take the weapon from her. "It's over, dear. You've saved us all."

Had she?

"She used the *macabre!*" someone yelled from the crowd.

"She nearly destroyed the arena!" Another waterbreaker added. "How do you explain that maelstrom?"

This time it was Belinda who rose fiercely. "She saved us all, you ungrateful fools!"

The arena erupted into arguments, waterbreaker against waterbreaker. Uncle Barrimond tried to keep the order, but it seemed impossible.

Mera's people both hated and loved her.

Mother was right. Perhaps, they weren't so different after all.

She studied Ariella's body, feeling jaded and numb. Mera had made a promise and she intended on keeping it.

Besides, the law was the law. Even if she was right to kill the queen, she had used the macabre. Which meant the merfolk had the right to claim her life.

Atlantea would always be the place where Mera's life began and ended. The place she loved and could never return to.

Pulling her triton away from Professor Currenter's grasp, she yanked it from her mother's body.

Ariella's gaping, lifeless eyes kept locked on Mera as her

body began to sink, but Mera grabbed her by her long red curls.

"I made a promise," she spoke quietly.

Death wasn't enough for her mother. The mad queen had to be buried on land, but not in the Isles of Fog, where they worshipped her.

No, she had to be buried where she was hated.

In dishonor. In shame.

Professor Currenter must have read her intentions, because panic overtook his semblance. "Mera, you will die. Please, let me speak to your uncle, and—"

"I know I'll die. Either way, I'm a walking corpse."

He blinked, his jaw hanging. "I can't let you go."

"I know that, too."

With one twist of her fingers, a wall of rushing water burst between them, and Mera boosted toward the forbidden zone, not caring to look back. If she did, she might lose her courage.

She hoped she would have enough time to bury Mother. If not, they'd burn into purple and black ashes together.

Somehow, that seemed very fitting.

CHAPTER 20

THE SANDSTONE STREET turned into a long promenade that
followed the shore.

Tir Na Nog's market stalls lined the path with brown, red,
and beige tents that matched perfectly with the amber path,
giving the entire area a touch of the Mediterranean—Mera
knew it from the pictures of Hakin and Rahal the Cap
showed her when she was a kid, and from the stories
Professor Currenter used to tell.

*"A Rahallian Moussaka is an explosion of flavor, my dear
princess."*

Getting to the Mediterranean nations was a problem,
though. The passage had to be made by Nightbringer, and
the prices were steep. Still, Mera promised herself she'd go
there one day, if only to taste that Moussaka.

Merchants yelled offers into the air, while Bast and Mera
walked down the path. Some stalls sold fruits, vegetables,
cheese, and meat as in any other market. Other merchants
however, offered spells, potions, and magical items such as a
mirror that could show one's true intentions, or a dagger
that would always hit the target.

In a borough brimming with magic, it often became a commodity.

Mera inhaled the salty tang of the ocean, a certain ache spreading in her chest. Clifftown was located one hour away from the sea, and sure, she could've visited, but what was the point if Mera couldn't enter the salty water without morphing into a siren?

An unnecessary suffering, really.

Just the scent of the sea made the longing in her chest squeeze harder.

"You okay, kitten?" Bast asked from beside her, a curious frown on his face.

"Great." She nodded absently. "So, how do we find this mad seer?"

Bast dodged a pudgy banshee in rags who held three kids. She yelled at them to behave as the older one escaped her grasp and dashed across the street.

"She's here most of the time," he said, watching the distancing banshee with amusement. "She's a confidential informant for Fallon. Most of her clientele is made of smugglers and small gangsters, so she knows a lot about what happens in the underworld."

"Really? Criminals take a psychic's vision as truth?"

"Kind of. Certain courts such as Autumn and Summer can be stupidly gullible. They like to check if their endeavors will be successful, so they get her blessing before going ahead."

"What if she says their *projects* won't work?"

"She never does. Never says they will, either. So, it doesn't matter if their plans work. In the end, the mad seer is always right."

"She's smart." And not the most reliable source of information out there.

Bast winked at her. "Faeries do appreciate a good old word play."

Very true.

They passed by two Sidhe females wearing flowing floral dresses, their hair pink and blue, their bodies moving with the elegance of gazelles. They eyed Bast with starving lust, but contrary to every other male on this street, he paid them no attention.

A light, fluttering sensation spread on Mera's chest.

"It's nonsense, if you ask me," he assured as they moved forward. "She's a seer. Pay her enough, and she'll tell you what you want to hear."

"It sucks a seer is our single lead," she grumbled. "We've been having a world of trouble because of stupid visions."

They passed by a brown tent with colorful knickknacks that called her attention, even if for a second.

"Want to grab a male's heart, madam?" The bearded merchant inside the tent quickly offered, showing her a round glass with purple liquid inside. "One drop, and he'll be all yours."

The siren strongly considered it, but Bast had already pulled his badge and shown it to him.

"You're selling love potions?" He put the badge back in his pocket. "Do you hate being a free faerie, *baku?*"

"Come on, officer." The fae smiled, but when he saw Bast wasn't joking around, fear bloomed in his face. "My apologies, sir!" He scrambled to put his potions away. "I'm so sorry, it won't happen again!"

Yeah, right. He'd probably move to another spot and keep selling that shit the moment they walked away.

"If I see you around here again, I'll take you down to the station." Bast stepped forward and grinned, displaying sharp canines. "You don't want to upset a nightling, do you?"

The man nodded shakily.

Bast stomped away, his shoulders slightly raised, his muscles clenched.

Mera followed him.

"He saw my uniform," he grumbled as they walked. "He knew I was an officer and he didn't care. He simply assumed I was corrupt like the rest of them."

"But you kind of are, Bast," she countered, though there was no way to put it simply. "You took Zev's phone. You murdered the witch and the bounty hunter."

Halting his steps, he turned to her, and his nostrils flared.

Her hands lifted in surrender. "I'm not saying you didn't *have* to do those things. I get where you were coming from, even though I don't approve. But you have to admit, you don't walk a straight line."

"Yes, but my goal, Fallon's goal, has always been establishing order." His tone was strained and heavy. "If that means we have to bend some rules here and there, I'm fine with it."

"I know," she agreed. "You bend the rules to solve cases. They bend the rules for their own interest. There's a world of difference."

He frowned at her, his jaw hanging open as if he couldn't believe how clearly she saw him. Yet, she did.

Bast was both chaotic and kind—if one was careful enough not to piss him off, that is. In his core, he might just be one of the best landriders Mera knew.

She stepped closer and wrapped her arms around his back, pressing her forehead against his chest. "You're doing your best, partner. That's all any of us can do."

She wanted to say so much more…

Mera was sorry for assuming he was an asshole when they'd first met—though to her own credit, Bast *was* kind of an asshole. She was sorry someone was out to kill him, and that he'd lost his father but couldn't mourn him—she knew that agony too well. She was sorry he'd spent years trying to bring justice to a corrupt borough, and that he'd lost Captain Asherath—for now—his only friend in this madness.

Bast hugged her back, the silence around them soothing, binding, somehow.

"Thanks, kitten," he whispered as he laid a hand on the back of her head. "Some partner you got, heh?"

"One of Hollowcliff's finest," she countered before stepping back.

They watched each other, a flurry of words hanging in the air around them. As Bast studied Mera, a soft smile hooked the corner of his lips—a tantalizing, extremely dangerous kind of smile that made her legs weak.

'Tell him,' her siren urged.

Tell him what?

'The truth.'

No. Never.

Sure, he was her partner, and such a bond demanded honesty, but she'd never told Jules, and she would never tell Bast either.

Still, in a fit of madness, her lips parted.

"Bast, I—"

"We should get going." Clearing his throat, he continued down the street.

A relieved sigh escaped Mera as her heartbeats drummed in her ears.

Saved by the bell.

They walked for a while in silence, until Bast stopped and stepped back. He observed a stall with a velvet red banner. Silver threads spelled "Madam Zukova" on the fabric.

He nudged Mera with his elbow, and pointed at an old Sidhe sitting behind the stall, facing another faerie.

The Sidhe had rosy hair, woven into a low braid that cascaded down her back. She was clad in a cerulean dress with golden embellishments on the hems, and gold jewelry shone at her wrists, neck, and ears.

"I think that's her," he whispered to Mera. "Fallon mentioned the mad seer was Spring Court."

Her semblance seemed to confirm it.

The old woman held on to her customer's hands, her eyes closed. The male faerie, Autumn Court if the bright red hair was any indication, watched her intently.

Bast opened his mouth to speak.

"Madam Zukova will attend to you soon," the woman cut him off, though her eyes remained closed.

Her thick, heavy accent was typical from the north. She might be Spring fae, but she hadn't been raised in Tir Na Nog.

"Give her red roses, yes?" she told the faerie sitting before her.

"That's it?" he asked with an incredulous grin. "She'll accept my marriage proposal, then?"

"The red of the roses signifies the red of her love. Madam Zukova does not lie." She opened her eyes and tapped his palms. "That will be twenty gold coins."

"Sixty dollars?" Mera asked. "Seriously? She didn't give you a proper answer!"

Madam Zukova's head snapped toward Mera, her eyes narrowed. "Silly humans. They do not understand how Danu works."

"Indeed," the Autumn Sidhe added. "Your undeveloped mind can never understand our ways."

Getting the coins from a pouch in his pocket, he handed them to Madam Zukova. He then kissed her hands, put on a brown fedora, and gave Mera the evil eye as he left.

"Maybe her clients are the mad ones," she whispered to Bast, and he held down a chuckle.

Madam Zukova leaned back in her chair and crossed her

legs. She watched Mera and Bast intently. "What do you want with me? Your start was not very good, yes?"

"My partner didn't mean to offend," Bast explained as he stepped in front of Mera, removing the badge from his pocket. "We'd like to ask you some questions, if that's all right? It's about Zev Ferris' murder."

Madam Zukova raised one eyebrow at him. "I heard they caught the killer of Zev."

"They caught a patsy," Mera retorted, stepping beside Bast. "Someone high up murdered the Summer King and infiltrated their henchman into Tir Na Nog police. We need to find out who."

Madam Zukova narrowed her eyes at Bast's badge. "I do not trust police. Criminals are more reliable."

"I'm a friend of Captain Asherath." He shoved the badge back in his pocket.

"Fallon can come to me himself, yes?" Before Bast could argue, she lifted her hand. "You say you're a friend of Fallon, but Fallon is not here to confirm. You understand, no?"

Considering the blatant corruption in the Tir Na Nog precinct, she was wise to doubt them.

Bast drew a sharp breath, letting it out slowly. "He's in a bit of a pickle at the moment. Finding Zev Ferris' killer will help Fallon." He made an X over his heart. "I guarantee it."

"Do you?" She observed Mera for a while, tapping her own chin. "You have something for me, girl?"

Okay, so she must have noticed Mera's body language. She couldn't have known she actually *did* have something for her.

In any case, Mera stepped closer and removed her phone from her jacket. She pressed play and put it close to Madam Zukova's ear.

After the fortuneteller heard Zev's recording, she gestured for them to sit on the two chairs that faced her.

"Zev was a fool. Good for business, but a fool either way." Shaking her head, she snorted. "The thing about fools, no? They tend to die before their time."

"Can you tell us anything about his death?" Bast pushed.

"He was in love. He asked if she loved him back." She shrugged carelessly. "I said the stars witnessed more impossible things. The foggy veil between Danu's realm and ours is thick, no?"

What a load of bullcrap.

Bast exchanged a worried glance with Mera.

"That's it?" he asked the seer. "That's everything you know?"

She nodded.

Leaning back in his chair, he slammed both hands on his face. "Back to square one."

Madam Zukova raised her hands with a shrug. "I cannot guess what the Summer King was thinking when he recorded that message. I'm seer, not miracle worker."

"What if you ask the dead?" Mera offered.

"I cannot."

"Indulge us."

The seer couldn't actually do it. No one could. But maybe Madam Zukova would remember something and claim it had been Zev's ghost who told her.

She observed Mera with cunning yellow eyes for a moment, seeing through her intentions. "Say I could peek through Danu's foggy veil. It's a pricey effort, yes?"

"Now we're talking." Bast snickered wickedly. "Ten gold coins."

She gave them a long grin that made her resemble a fox, then showed them her palm. "Fifty, please."

"Twenty."

"Fifty."

Madam Zukova was perfectly aware she had the upper hand.

"We're not paying you one hundred and fifty dollars before you tell us something," Mera grumbled.

"Then you may leave." Madam Zukova showed them the exit. "Do not forget girl, I am a scoundrel, yes?"

Grunting a curse under his breath, Bast removed a hundred-dollar bill from his pocket and handed it to her. "Make our time worth it and you get the rest."

She winced as she grabbed the note, shoving it inside the top of her dress. "Human money is so dirty." She wiped her fingers on the fabric. "Gold is much cleaner. Prettier too, no?"

"Yeah, sure," Mera said. "So, why did Zev think you could help us?"

"I do not know. I must see first." Closing her eyes, she relaxed her shoulders.

The humming of a low tune arose from deep within her chest, a continuing droning sound that had to belong somewhere within the trenches—or the fiery hell most humans feared.

She suddenly stopped, her body going incredibly still.

"Treachery of the blood," she announced. "Poseidon's child is dead."

A shiver coursed down Mera's spine.

Poseidon's child...

Her mother's cruel grin flashed in her mind, her voice echoing in Mera's ears. *"You still doubt me, daughter?"*

Mera chortled as she glanced at Bast. "It's a joke, right?"

"There was someone named Poseidon in Sara Hyland's notebook," he whispered. "I can't believe I'm saying this, but the mad seer gave us a good clue, kitten."

Panic overwhelmed Mera's senses. She wanted to run and

never come back, a cold sweat breaking through her pores. This had to be a lie, or a fucking, awful coincidence.

There's a logical explanation, she told herself.

"Analyze what's before you," the Captain's voice echoed in her mind. *"Always trust the facts, cookie."*

Okay. Deep breath.

Poseidon didn't exist, so he couldn't father children.

Inhale. Exhale.

Mera shoved her panic deep inside, because she couldn't afford to lose her mind, especially now.

She watched Madam Zukova, the old woman's body stiff as stone.

Poseidon's child... The sentence reverberated in her mind nonstop, loud, screeching, until she felt someone pressing her hand.

"Kitten? You all right?"

Nodding hastily, she took a settling breath. "Fine."

Bast's incredulous look said he didn't believe her, but Mera didn't know what else to say.

There has to be an explanation.

There has to be.

"Treachery of the blood," Madam Zukova repeated, then went deadly silent for a while.

Mera was about to ask if she was okay, when the seer inhaled deeply. Turning to Mera, she smiled with her eyes closed. "Is that you, my little fry?"

Bile thrashed in Mera's stomach, and she feared she might throw up at any moment. "Whatever you're doing, stop," she warned.

"It is you! My dear princess, I'm so glad!"

This wasn't possible. It couldn't be him. And even if it was, Madam Zukova spoke to the dead, *allegedly*, which meant...

No, no, no.

He couldn't be dead.

Mera shook her head, tears brimming in the corner of her eyes. "I have no clue how you're doing this, you cheap psychic bastard, but—"

"Don't blame the messenger," Madam Zukova frowned, but kept her eyes closed. "It's me, little fry. Don't you remember?" She smiled sweetly. "Tell me, my dear. Have you tasted that delicious Moussaka I told you about?"

"How could you know that!" She bellowed more than asked as she stood from her chair, but the seer didn't reply.

Mera held a whimper, breathing becoming harder and harder. She put a hand over her mouth, yet she couldn't speak, just cry.

Bast's jaw was set as he observed Mera and the seer. "Who are you?" he asked.

Madam Zukova turned to him, her mouth shaping an 'O'. "You're not alone, princess?"

"No," Mera replied, nearly choking with tears.

"I see."

"Professor," she dared, a piercing ache spreading in her chest, "is that really you? Are you dead?"

A loud huff blew through Madam Zukova's lips. "Nonsense. I'm using Ursula as a channel. We've been searching for you for so long... Ever since she had a vision you were alive."

Relief washed over Mera. She thanked all Gods everywhere—human, fae, Atlantean, it didn't matter.

Bast ogled Mera with suspicion, but she couldn't come up with an explanation, not now.

"I-I…" she couldn't speak. She didn't know what to say or think. "I've missed you so much, but I couldn't come back. You have to understand. After everything that happened, everything I did, I couldn't—"

Madam Zukova leaned forward. "I understand, dear." A

certain gloom took over the seer's face, and she turned to the side as if listening to someone. Finally, she nodded. "We don't have much time." She stood and cupped Mera's cheek, like she was seeing Mera clearly although her eyelids were shut. "I hope you're happy there. Happier than you ever were here."

She cupped the seer's hand and pressed it closer. "I am. And I'll have that moussaka one day."

With you, professor. I promise.

"What a wonderful dream." Madam Zukova tapped her cheek gently, the way Professor Currenter used to when she was a merling. "Now that I know you're alive, I can rest. Your friend Belinda will be most pleased to hear about this." The seer's expression fell, her shoulders dropping. "Before I go, though, promise me you'll never attempt to come back, my dear."

Mera frowned. She wasn't planning on returning, but something seemed off. "Are you all right?"

"We're fine." Madam Zukova leaned forward and kissed her forehead. "Grow strong, Mera."

Fear edged the professor's tone, she could sense it through the mad seer's voice.

"Why?"

Madam Zukova's eyes spread so wide Mera could see the golden specks in her yellow irises. She inhaled deeply and bent backwards, like she'd been underwater for a long time.

Maybe she had been.

Pointing one quivering finger at Mera, she bent over and coughed. "Remarkable," she managed, drawing in deep breaths. "Oh, you precious, precious thing."

Bast stood, placing himself between them. "Kitten, what's going on?"

Mera and the seer exchanged a worried glance, then

Madam Zukova swallowed, taking one long, steadying breath.

"That was her grandfather," she lied.

Mera couldn't say why the fae covered for her, especially when no favors had been involved, but she was grateful, nonetheless.

Bast frowned. "I thought you were an orphan?"

"Kind of," Mera said vaguely, her throat tightening. "I had an abusive mother. I escaped, and never looked back."

A world of questions crowded his blue eyes. "But you called him 'professor'. And he called you *princess*."

"Bast, I can't go over all of that now." Her voice came out ragged and weak. "We have to focus on our case."

"Mera—"

"Please?"

He observed her for a moment, confusion in his stare. Finally, he nodded, respecting the line she'd drawn.

She couldn't thank him enough.

"Treachery of the blood," he said. "Are you thinking what I'm thinking?"

She nodded. "We have to pay the Summer Court a visit."

CHAPTER 21

"We have to be smart," Mera said as she walked in circles around Bast's living room. "The light courts own Tir Na Nog. Even if we had hard evidence to arrest Lisandra or Zachary—which we don't—the moment we enter your precinct with them, we'll be the ones behind bars."

"All fun things are a bit mad," Bast countered with his eyes closed.

He sat on the sofa with his legs crossed, hands over his knees. He seemed relaxed and peaceful.

Mera resented him a little. How could he be so calm, considering what they were about to face?

"Have you reached Captain Asherath yet?" she asked.

"Fallon arrived in Clifftown. Your Captain says hi, by the way."

"Say hi back." She slammed both hands on her waist. "Does she know how we can arrest Zev's murderer and keep them behind bars?"

He opened his eyes and smiled. "Actually, she does."

They knocked on the white wooden door of the Summer King's penthouse. A pixie with golden hair, and a golden maid's uniform opened it for them.

"Could you fetch your missus?" Bast asked. "Tell her it's urgent."

The pixie gave him a short curtsy and went away. Not ten seconds passed before queen bitch stormed into the vast living room in a knee-length golden dress, her nostrils flared, her cheeks a rosy red that nearly matched the color of her hair.

"How dare you step into my home unannounced!" She pointed a finger at Bast, ignoring Mera's presence. "Is Captain Cane aware you're here?"

"Solomon is not my Captain," Bast replied simply, removing a pair of cuffs from his pocket. "And you, Lisandra Ferris, are under arrest for your husband's murder."

She gaped at them. "What?"

Bast went to put on the cuffs, but she waved him away, angry golden sparkles whipping in the air between them. "Don't you dare, Sebastian."

He rubbed the bridge of his nose, then flicked his hand. A circle of void blinked from thin air, and it sucked in the golden sparkles at once. The darkness remained, hanging midair as stars glittered against the void.

A silent threat.

Lisandra gulped, and when Bast moved to cuff her again, she didn't put up a fight.

As soon as the cuffs locked shut, an iron pin clicked away from the surface and touched her skin, voiding her magic—a cleverly made device that allowed faeries to arrest other fae without losing their own power in the process.

"Are you daft?" Lisandra wriggled against the cuffs as if regretting her decision to comply, but it was pointless now.

"You dare barge into my house and accuse me of my husband's murder!" The high pitch in her tone pierced Mera's ears. "That's illegal!"

"Considering how *your* court runs this borough," Mera said, "you have no fucking clue of what illegal means, lady."

She snorted. "This is ridiculous. I'll see that you pay for this, human! As for you, Prince of Night, I'll have your head on a platter come morning!"

Bast raised an eyebrow at Mera. "That sounds a lot like contempt to authority, doesn't it, Detective Maurea?"

"It sure does, Detective Dhay."

"I guess I'll add it to the murder charge."

Lisandra screamed, her head puffing in anger. "How dare you!"

"What's going on?" Zachary stepped into the living room.

His straight hair was disheveled and his shirt open. A blue-skinned sprite with black hair followed him, and when she saw the scene, she scurried out of the apartment.

Mera raised her gun with one hand, taking the cuffs from inside her jacket with the other. "Zachary Ferris, you are under arrest for your father's murder."

He stepped back with a confused frown. "Are you out of your minds? You can't arrest us. You have no evidence!"

"Oh, we've got evidence," she assured. "I strongly advise you to comply."

"You do?" Realization dawned on him, and his shocked demeanor morphed into nonchalance. "You went to the mad seer. I hardly see how a psychic's words qualify as evidence."

Bingo.

"Quiet, Zachary!" Lisandra ordered.

"I'm curious." He strolled around the living room as if Mera didn't have an iron bullet aimed at his head. "What did Madam Zukova tell you?"

"That you did it," Bast baited him, holding a bewildered Lisandra by her arm.

"That's easy," he shrugged. "Did she tell you why?"

Lisandra stopped trying to break free. "Zachary, what are you talking about?"

"I killed Father." He admitted carelessly. "It was bad enough that he cheated on you with everything that had curves. But when I found out he was keeping his pregnant, human whore here, in our court—right under our noses—I had to do something." He ran a hand over his hair. "The scandal alone…"

Bast had been so right about that giant asshole.

"It was for the best," Zachary explained. "With my leadership, we'll break ties with those abominable humans and take over Tir Na Nog, then Hollowcliff. Soon, Tagrad will belong to the fittest and strongest." His eyes glinted wickedly as he focused on Mera. "The courts will rule the land, and humans will be our slaves."

"Ah, so it wasn't just about the scandal. It was also a coup," Bast concluded, his tone flat. "Call me impressed. Let me guess, Autumn and Spring happily approve your ascendance to the Summer throne."

Zachary watched him with amusement. "Of course they do. We run this city, Dhay. And your precinct."

Mera clicked her gun and wiggled the cuffs with her free hand, throwing them on the sofa for him. "Do me a favor and cuff yourself, will you?"

"Afraid I'll use magic against you, Detective?" The tip of his tongue licked his lips, taunting her.

"Just keeping a safe distance. You *are* a murderous bastard, after all." She nodded to her own gun. "I don't need to tell you these are iron bullets, right?"

"You don't." He glanced at the cuffs as he calmly sat on the sofa. "In my defense, at the time I thought the child was my father's." Crossing his arms, he sighed. "Foolish, I'll admit. I was taken by rage and couldn't think straight. I'm sure you know what that's like, don't you, Dhay?"

Bast ignored his attempt of getting under his skin. "You can use that argument in your trial, but I call it bullshit. Now, why did you drown Sara Hyland?"

"You won't believe me if I tell you."

Narrowing his eyes, Bast cocked his head to the right. "Try me."

"I followed her one day, ready to end her before things got out of hand," he answered carefully. Slowly. "She went to the beach and stood on the sand, watching the waves. I approached from behind, but she didn't notice my presence. I was about to grab her when she yelled into the ocean, 'You can't have my baby!'"

Mera felt as if she were falling within herself. *Poseidon's child* rang in her head repeatedly.

"Did she seem mentally unstable to you?" Bast prodded.

It was a possibility. One Mera had to believe in, because the alternative... the alternative didn't make any sense.

"Unstable? No. Simply a gold-digging whore, trying to scam my father." His long fingers brushed his chin thought-fully, as he stared out of the open archways that led into the outside balcony. "For a split second, I could swear I spotted a silver stingray with neon-blue eyes watching her from the water. But then I blinked, and it was gone." He clicked his tongue. "Pity, really. I would have enjoyed capturing it."

Mera might've lost the ability to breathe altogether.

Mother's technology...

Someone was using it to communicate with Sara Hyland.

Zachary stood and went to a golden table. He poured an amber liquid from a fine crystal bottle into a glass.

"That's when I heard it, of course." After taking a long

gulp, he hissed through his teeth. "It wasn't like a thought; it was as if someone else talked to me with my own voice." He raised his glass at Bast. "Your kind is good with mind tricks, but this... this puts your abilities to shreds. I can't say how I knew someone spoke to me, I just did. Which meant I had lost my mind, but who cares? There have been mad kings before."

His hand trembled slightly.

"What did this voice tell you?" Mera asked, following his every move, her aim sharp and ready. She pointed it to the sofa's cushions and the cuffs atop them, then back at him. "Also, if you don't mind."

He ignored her request. "The voice told me to give the human's soul to the sea." Drinking until the glass was empty, he slammed it back on the table. "So, I did. I stupefied the human and dragged her to the water."

"You don't strike me as the type who gets his hands dirty," Bast challenged.

"Usually, I'm not," he countered simply, his gaze lost.

"Your father had affairs before," Lisandra mumbled, her voice quivering with shock and sorrow. "Why was this any different?"

"It was a filthy human, Mother! The banshees, the pixies —those affairs I could forgive. But one of these weak, disgusting bugs?" He pointed at Mera. "Never! Spring and Autumn would think us weak! It would shift the entire power balance. I couldn't let it happen." A deep breath made its way down his lungs, and he studied the floor aimlessly. "I held the human underwater... bubbles popped on the surface until there were none left. I waited a little longer after that."

"You ended her life and her child's," Mera stated, something knotting in her throat. "You went for your father next."

Walking to the window, he watched the city, holding his hands behind his back. "The human dropped her bag when I stupefied her. Father would be tracking her through that ridiculous device he'd bought. I saw an opportunity to make him suffer, *and* to reach my own goals. I paid a faerie to winnow me and the body into Clifftown, dropped it at the human's home and waited, knowing father would take the bait."

When he turned to them, Mera thought she might be losing it, but she spotted regret in his eyes.

"Father was powerful, so I had no choice. The moment he entered the apartment and found her, I had to take advantage. I grabbed the pointiest object I could find. He pivoted in time to see me, but not fast enough to stop me. I rammed the stake into his chest." He scoffed. "So powerful and almighty that he was. So disappointed in me as he stopped breathing."

Bast exchanged one worried glance with Mera. "I think now's the time you cuff yourself." He raised one hand, and flames of void whipped from his skin. "I can always force you to surrender. That would be fun."

"I murdered Zev," Lisandra blurted, her voice a whisper as tears trailed down her cheeks. "My son is trying to protect me."

"Stop, Mother. They won't make an arrest. There's no evidence to incriminate me and Solomon is a good friend." He snapped his fingers and some twenty Sidhe, wearing fighting leathers, barged into the space.

"You're threatening two officers," Bast growled.

"Who do you think got rid of Captain Asherath?" A diabolical grin cut through his lips. "The Autumn Court was mightily grateful for my assistance."

Bast's teeth gritted in anger. "*Sakala wu, malachai.*"

"I'd let my mother go, if I were you." The prince turned into a golden blur and boosted toward Mera. He tossed her gun aside and trapped her in a headlock before she could react. "I won't ask again."

Ignoring the strain on her neck, she laughed. "You're toast, assface."

Only then did he truly pay attention to her.

Zachary patted her waist with one hand and found the wiretap Mera had been using. Pulling it away from her, he yanked the duct tape that attached the device to her skin. It burned, but only for a quick second.

"What's this?" he threw the tap on the floor and stepped on it.

"It's a listening device," Bast explained. "Hollowcliff task-forces will be paying you a visit soon. Your puppet at the precinct can only buy you so much time."

Zev closed his arms around Mera's neck. "You're lying."

Bast shrugged. "You think you can fight humans and their guns. You might be right, but it's a serious gamble. You forget, however, that Tir Na Nog is a part of Hollowcliff. Even if your little coup worked, you'd never take down shifters, vampires, and witches. We're stronger together, remember that, *malachai?*" He chuckled low in his chest. "Your little dream has always been a delusion."

"*Rae-henai!*" The Summer Prince snapped. "The two of you won't leave here alive."

The faeries closed in on Bast, some with crackling magic bursting around their bodies, others unsheathing daggers and swords from their belts.

Twenty against one.

Mera writhed against Zachary's grip, but he was too strong. "You coward!"

He chuckled lowly in his chest. "You'll have a front-row seat to your partner's end, human. Consider yourself lucky."

Letting go of a shocked and unresponsive Lisandra, Bast

stepped away from the Summer Queen. The faeries followed his every move, ready to strike.

Clouds of night flared out from his hands. Grinning widely at the Sidhe around him, he flashed them his sharp fangs.

"Let's dance, *malachais*."

CHAPTER 22

THE FIRST FAERIE sent a whip of red magic at Bast. It wrapped around his forearm, crackling and sizzling. He winced in pain but pulled the Sidhe toward him and smacked a beautiful punch on his nose. The magic vanished into thin air as the faerie crumpled unconscious to the floor.

Flames of night circled around Bast's feet, whipping out and burning any opponent who approached, but these Sidhe were powerful. Their own magic battled Bast's darkness as they jumped into the circle, weapons at hand.

It wasn't fair.

Mera struggled to break free from Zachary, while Bast fought every faerie that attacked him. Her partner was already panting, and several cuts ripped across his shirt and vest. A small mound of unconscious faeries lay to his left.

Zachary was strong, too strong, which meant he must be enhancing his strength through magic.

"You'll watch, human," he whispered as three faeries jumped at Bast at the same time.

'The last person who said that to me paid with her life,' her siren growled.

Two of the faeries unsheathed their swords, pressing the blades across his neck in an X, while the third shot golden light into the flaming darkness surrounding him. Bast screamed in pain as a hissing sound bloomed from the clash, as if the Summer fae's magic was scorching his own.

His flames of night wavered before sinking into the floor.

Another Sidhe grabbed the handcuffs from the sofa and clicked them around Bast's wrists. Four faeries to contain one.

Fucking unfair.

The guard stepped away carefully, observing him.

Bast growled, veins popping on his forehead since he probably tried to use his magic, but the tentacles of night didn't show. He glared at Zachary, his chest heaving, teeth clenched. "You'll regret this."

"Will I?" Zachary shrugged. "Doesn't seem that way."

One of the Summer faeries unsheathed the sword on his belt, breaking Lisandra's cuffs in half. She rubbed her wrists as the cuffs clinked to the ground.

The Summer Queen watched Bast with sorrow before facing her son. "Zachary, you've proved your point. But there's no defeating Tagrad, and there's no defeating the police that will soon storm into our home. You must run."

Mera blinked, wondering if she was dreaming. For the first time ever, Lisandra seemed... rational.

"We control the police," Zachary snapped. "Our court is mighty. We *are* Tir Na Nog, and Tagrad obeys our every whim."

"We can bend the law, but there's a limit, and you've crossed it." Tears burdened her voice. "There's no return from this, son."

"You clueless bitch!" he barked. "No wonder father cheated on you."

Lisandra gasped, but Zachary was done with her. He

218

focused on Bast, who still struggled against his cuffs. "How does it feel to be helpless, Detective Dhay?"

"I don't know," he countered. "Why don't you tell me?"

A smirk grazed Zachary's lips. "Stay," he whispered in Mera's ear.

His magic became a physical hold on her, weighing the same as a hundred iron shackles, trying to drag her to the center of the Earth.

The bastard had stupefied her.

Her own magic, born from the water inside her, thrashed against his, but his spell was a wall she couldn't break.

Zachary strolled toward Bast with hands behind his back. He stopped before him, briefly turning to Mera. "I've been waiting to do this for a long time."

His fist violently smashed into Bast's stomach, and her partner fell on both knees, gasping for air. Zachary didn't wait. He kicked Bast's face, the thick, hollow sound piercing Mera's chest.

Her partner slouched on the marbled floor.

"Stop!" she screamed, but Zachary didn't listen.

"I lost count of the times you and your Captain Asherath busted my court's dealings." He kicked Bast in the stomach again, lifting him in the air for a second before he crashed back against the floor. Breaths wheezed from Bast's throat, clawing into Mera's chest.

"Is that all you got, you *shig*?" He coughed, spitting dark, wine-red blood.

Grinning, Zachary ran a hand through his straight hair. "I'm only getting started, Detective Dhay."

Bast struggled to push himself up, and the Summer Prince watched him with amusement. His legs shook beneath him, but they didn't buckle.

"You're mighty brave when I'm wearing these." Bast half-turned to show him his cuffs. "Why not make it a fair fight?"

Zachary's answer was a left jab on his ribs, then his jaw. He hit Bast nonstop, the sound of his knuckles against his flesh a cruel *thwack, thwack, thwack!*

Angry tears soaked Mera's cheeks. She howled and thrashed, but her body didn't move.

Dark blood streamed down the right side of Bast's face. It tainted his disheveled hair, dripping over his shirt and vest. He wobbled on his feet but refused to fall, like a stubborn tree nearly cut in half.

Bast spat onto Zachary's fancy shoes. "Rot in the deepest crevices of Danu's hells, *baku.*"

The Summer Prince raised his hand for another blow; perhaps the final one.

Mera couldn't take it anymore. Fury scorched through her body, her soul, *all of her*, making her see burning red. "Touch him again, and I'll end you!" she shouted.

Zachary gave her a smirk. "I have an idea."

Walking closer, he trapped Mera in another headlock, his magic freeing her enough that she could fight against his grip.

Not that it was any help.

A laugh rumbled in his chest, pressing on Mera's spine. He forced his cheek against hers, but kept focusing on Bast. "You'll watch your pretty human die, Dhay. How does that sound?"

"Your fight is with me!" Bast boomed, panic lashing in his blue eyes as he stepped forward. Instantly, two blades criss-crossed before his neck in a warning, but he fought against them, causing thin lines of blood to trickle down his skin. "If you hurt her, I swear—"

"You swear what?" Zachary laughed. "You're powerless, Detective."

Mera didn't know why or how, but a familiar sizzling took over her body. The raw power she hadn't felt since the day she'd killed her mother, swam underneath her skin, clawing into her veins. The hairs on the nape of her neck rose.

'Show them the power of your song...'

"Let me go, you fucking asshole," Mera ordered.

Zachary's magic shattered against the tsunami that was hers. His heart went suddenly still. She could feel it as the macabre spread into his blood, quietly, silently. He hadn't noticed it yet, his focus more on Mera's glamour than anything else.

Zachary's arms trembled as he lowered them. With a scowl, he grudgingly stepped aside. "How are you doing this?"

"Quiet."

Mera felt the rush of blood through his veins, the clenching of his jaw, the rise and fall of his lungs. All of him was stamped into the macabre, all of him a map in front of her.

Pushing against her magic, Zachary tried to mumble a kill order, but his jaw set itself before he could finish.

The goons around Mera and Bast blinked, as if they couldn't quite grasp what was happening. They did get the message, though.

"For Summer!" they yelled, brandishing their weapons.

Time seemed to slow when the two Sidhe beside her partner raised their swords, the blades cutting the air toward his neck.

Bast's gentle, warm gaze was an apology. He smiled softly, a silent message that said he cared for her; the same message that told her to look away. That he didn't want Mera to see him die; not like this.

Mera felt trapped between reality and nightmare as the macabre burst from her—straight into the two faeries.

More, it whispered, *I want more.*

Her magic went further and deeper, plunging into every Sidhe warrior's essence, all twenty of them. It pierced into their entrails, controlled the water in their tear ducts, and took over their flesh, making it hers to command.

Mera exhaled in relief as Bast's executioners stopped mid-swoop.

They stared at each other, clueless to what had happened. Their magic fought against her control, but Mera was a giant and they were nothing but ants.

This thing inside her scared Mera and her siren, but it also freed them like nothing else in the world.

Zachary glared at her, his face nearly as red as Lisandra's hair. "Abomina-tion," he managed through his clenched jaw.

Remarkable that he could speak, really.

He struggled against her power enough to grunt, "*Akritana.*"

Waterbreaker.

Stating the obvious wouldn't help him, though. Mera surveyed the room that now belonged to her.

Every Sidhe shook against her control, trying to fight the macabre. Which was pointless. These fae might be powerful, but Mera's surge was bigger than them, bigger than anything, including herself.

'Something's wrong...' her own voice warned from a great distance inside her.

Mera wiggled her fingers and the faeries' blood boiled. Maybe they hadn't been alive during the war, but they must've heard the tales of entire armies exploding in a symphony of flesh and bone.

The macabre's dance.

Their bodies inflated, the sheer pain from torn veins and flesh driving them mad. Mera knew because the macabre showed her *everything*. They screamed, and some even pissed themselves.

Lisandra curled into a corner on the far left, and stared in horror as her skin puffed, her eyes nearly popping out of their sockets.

She's innocent, Mera's muffled voice fought through her raging trance.

I do not care.

Apart from Bast, she would burst every fae in this place from the inside out, and be reborn in their blood. It was Mera's to claim.

That annoying voice⎯her own⎯spoke again, but this time, it didn't whisper. It shrieked, bellowing one word repeatedly inside her head.

Mother! Mother! Mother!

Mera gasped and stepped back. She stared at her own hands, still reeling in that raw, larger-than-life power. The metallic taste of blood spread over her tongue, sumptuous and enticing.

'Free me,' her own voice whispered. *'Free yourself.'*

Never. Never again.

Bast gaped at the swollen Sidhe while they slowly deflated. "Kitten?" he croaked, turning to her.

Mera stared at the faeries circling them, Zachary included. She'd made a garden of crying, pissing, terrified flesh statues. Her macabre still held them tightly in place, but they didn't seem to be in pain anymore.

'They will tell on us,' her siren warned. *'Kill them.'*

They deserved it, especially Zachary, but Lisandra didn't. The Summer Queen might be a bitch, but she had no blame in this. And Mera had nearly killed her.

Slamming both hands over her face, she finally claimed control over her thoughts. Poseidon in the trenches, she'd almost...

So much for helping the innocent.

These faeries had become witnesses of her true nature; of

what she could do. Yes, it was either their lives or hers now, but mass-murdering went against everything Mera fought for as a detective; everything the Cap taught her.

To protect and serve.

When she'd fought her mother, Mera was also protecting and serving. Her people. All of Atlantea. Perhaps, that had been her purpose all along. Yet, ending the faeries' lives would turn her into a monster.

Mera would rather die than to make Ariella Wavestorm proud.

"I guess you won't need to report me, partner," she whispered, hands falling at her sides, her throat hoarse and her tone weak. "Their testimonies will be enough."

Bast stumbled toward her, a wine-red trickle coming down the edge of his mouth. Half of his face was painted with his own blood, the other swollen and going purple. He wiggled his wrists behind him and Mera got the message.

Raising her hand, she pointed at him. Tears pushed out of every fae's body at her silent command, especially Zachary's. They screamed in pain, but she didn't care. Not after what they'd done to Bast.

Their teardrops concentrated into a tiny mass of salty water that floated before her, then morphed into a line that entered the locks in Bast's cuffs.

Mera calmed the water.

The molecules which made the liquid thrummed slower, until water turned to ice. It broke through the lock easily, the cuffs clicking as they hit the marbled floor.

"You used magic on a cuff," Bast spoke with a certain awe. "That's impossible."

Yeah, no shit, but Mera couldn't explain how she'd done it. She had no clue how she'd done a lot of things today.

Bast stepped forward, pressing his forehead to hers, his hands carefully settling on her waist. "I knew you were *akri-*

tana the moment you used the macabre on that witch, kitten. I'm not stupid."

"Why didn't you report me?" She stared at him.

A soft smile pulled at his lips, and he nudged the tip of her nose with his. "I'm your partner. Isn't that part of the deal?"

"Not particularly." She held the cry that pushed out of her. "Thank you, Bast. You bought me a few days."

Mera wouldn't live for much longer. The police would put an iron bullet in her head the moment they got there, but she was thankful to have shared her last case with him.

"You need to run," he said quietly.

Mera strongly considered it. But then... "I have nowhere to go. If I return to the ocean, I'm as good as dead. I don't want to live as a fugitive, always looking over my shoulder until you, the Cap, or Jules is forced to kill me."

Waterbreaker or not, Mera couldn't outrun a witch's tracking spell, a shifter's sense of smell, or a vampire's hearing. Sooner or later, she would be found.

"I won't make the people in my precinct do that. I won't make *you* do that." Her heart squeezed, and she took in a deep breath. "Promise me something?"

His pained eyes peered into hers, as if he were seeing Mera for the first time. "Anything."

"Will you look after the Cap and Jules?" She bit her bottom lip, holding the need to cry. "Please?"

He cupped her cheek and leaned down, his breath shy and warm against hers until their lips touched.

Bast's fingers dug onto her hair as he pulled her closer, deepening their kiss. Mera took him, all of him, his hungry lips and panted breaths infusing fire and life into her. The taste of his warm tongue grazed hers, and a bit of his blood too, but she didn't care.

Wrapping her arms around his neck, she pushed herself against him, their breaths rapid and shallow as their tongues battled in a sensual war, their bodies tangled in a perfect tune. Right then, consumed by his embrace, she figured there was no better way to go.

As far as last kisses went, that one took the prize.

Bast pulled back and brushed a lock of hair off her face, gazing down at her with glistening blue eyes. Even hurt and covered in a great deal of his own blood, he looked incredibly handsome.

"Remember me like this, Mera." He pecked her lips lightly. "I'll do anything to save you. Even if it means you'll hate me."

Mera frowned, not understanding what he meant. "Shut up and kiss me again, *baku*," she teased, yet instead of doing it, Bast stepped back.

She tried to reach for him, but something held her in place.

A void with shining stars had risen from the ground, tangling around her wrists and ankles. She tried to lift her hand, but the tentacles clung to her like tar.

"Bast? What the hell?"

Ignoring her, he walked toward the Sidhe in silence. All twenty of them. When he grasped a sword from the floor, his black flames engulfed the blade.

"Bast!" she yelled, but he didn't listen; didn't hesitate as he cut through the first faerie's neck, then the next, and the next.

Bast moved like shadows, fast and nearly unseen.

A pitch-black blur.

The faeries gurgled as blood drooled from the cuts down to their chests, yet they couldn't fall because her macabre lingered inside them. As she pulled it back, the bodies dropped harshly, their hollow thumps against the marble echoing around her.

Mera's power swirled in her core, ready to stop Bast, but

she couldn't will it forward, even though she tried. Shock and horror froze her as she watched.

Maybe he didn't need those tentacles to hold her in place. The bloodshed ahead was enough.

Coming to herself in time to remove her power from the remaining faeries, she gave them a fighting chance. Nevertheless, Bast was swift and merciless. Even if they could fight him, he killed them as easily as one would cut through paper.

Some he ended with the blade, others with spears of void that cut through air and flesh. His night swallowed a fae on the right, leaving a rusty skeleton behind.

On and on he went, until there were only two fae left breathing.

Zachary and Lisandra.

"Bast…" Mera muttered.

The white marbled floor was slick with fae blood.

His head snapped left, into the empty hallway. "If you speak of what you saw here today, I will come for you. You've seen what I can do."

Silence replied.

"Leave, or you die with them," he pushed.

Two maids came into view, shaking in terror. Hastily nodding, they scurried away while Lisandra crouched on the floor, whimpering, and hiding her face between her knees.

Across from her, Zachary glared at Bast. The Summer Prince screamed as golden light shone from his fists.

He barged at Bast, but her partner easily dodged the attack.

While they fought, Mera felt weakened and half asleep. She faintly noticed the blurs of light and darkness clashing furiously ahead.

Glancing down at the tentacles of void around her wrist and ankles, she realized they were doing this to her. They were draining her magic.

Her consciousness, too.

She pushed the macabre toward Zachary and Bast. Someone had to stop them, but her magic didn't lurch forward. She could hardly feel it at all.

Bast's sword dropped to the ground, but he and the Summer Prince went on, fighting hand-to-hand, golden and black auras beaming around them. Their magic moved as fluidly as their strikes, and even though they were battling, Mera couldn't help but compare it to a sort of dance.

In one quick move, Bast punched Zachary, who punched him in return. Their forms started to blur.

Mera's head felt awfully light. She forced herself to focus, right when the golden form fell on his knees.

"Fine! I surrender!" Zachary called for a truce, offering Bast his wrists. "Take me to your precinct."

"The Autumn and Spring Courts will find a way to bail you," her partner's tone was freezing cold. "You'll go unpunished."

"I'm giving myself in, Dhay." He sneered. "You're an officer. You must arrest me."

"You know it's your only way out," he growled. "You'll be freed in no time, and then you'll testify against Mera."

Zachary gulped. "I swear I won't!"

"Your word means shit, *baku*."

"Bast…" she mumbled, narrowing her eyes. She couldn't see his face clearly. "He's surrendering. You can't hurt him."

Her partner became a blur of shadows, and Mera heard a sound akin to wood snapping. Zachary's foggy form slumped on the floor.

Bast approached a screaming, red-haired ball, curling on the corner.

"No," Mera muttered. "She didn't know."

"Lisandra saw you," that cold tone replied.

That wasn't her partner. It couldn't be.

Mera's vision came to focus enough to see the tears scrolling down Bast's cheeks; the pitch black of his eyes. "Don't…"

"You didn't run away," he told Mera. "I had no choice."

"There's always a choice," she managed through her haze. Her thoughts didn't connect, didn't make any sense. "Bast, I love you, but you just killed everyone."

He grumbled a curse under his breath. "You could've picked a better time to say that, kitten."

"What?" Her eyelids felt so heavy. "That you're a murderer?"

"I've known that for a while." He ran a hand through his hair. "So, you love me?"

His words carried sound but hardly any meaning. She blinked, barely able to force her eyes open. "Do I?"

He stepped closer.

Considering what he could do, how powerless he'd rendered her, Mera should be terrified. But she wasn't. At all.

Damned the old gods, she even craved for his touch.

His lips pressed a kiss on her forehead, belonging to her partner once again, and not that ruthless… the words from the bounty hunter flashed in her mind.

Death bringer.

"Sleep," Bast ordered.

"You killed the witch… to keep my secret," she managed, pushing through the drowsiness that swallowed her. "You knew she wasn't a threat to my life. You were protecting me."

"Maybe," Bast answered with a shrug, then stepped away, toward the corner of the room.

Lisandra bawled. "Please, Sebastian! No!"

I have to help her, Mera told herself. *Have to keep awake.* Still, she couldn't discern what happened around her anymore.

"I'll never forgive you," she slurred before her legs gave in, but something cushioned her fall.

Night. It spread beneath her and laid her carefully on the floor, its touch warm and gentle like Bast's own.

"I'll never ask you to," he said quietly.

Once Mera's eyes closed, she couldn't open them again. Lisandra's horrid screams faded into a lullaby, then into nothing at all.

CHAPTER 23

"Bast!" Mera gasped, jolting awake.

She stared at a wooden ceiling, her fingers digging into a leather sofa. Sitting up, she realized she was in a Captain's office, though she couldn't tell if it might be Ruth's or Asherath's.

Ah wait, white leather sofa. Asherath's then. Well, technically, the office belonged to that bastard Solomon Cane.

Mera was alone, and a silly, irrational part of her missed Bast—even if she felt both relieved and disheartened that he wasn't there. She rubbed her forehead, feeling an oncoming headache.

Mera hated how much she missed him, how cold and lonely she felt when he wasn't there, even after everything he'd done.

The door opened and the Cap entered.

Her Cap.

A wide grin spread on her lips when she saw Mera awake, intensifying the crow's feet near her eyes.

Mera held back the indignity of crying, but fuck, how she'd missed Ruth.

The Cap sat down beside her, trapping her in a bear hug that squeezed the air out of her lungs. "I'm so glad you're okay, cookie."

Mera hugged her back, still a little dazed. "What happened?"

"So much." She let her go, and cupped her cheeks.

Today she was less Captain and more Ruth, the woman who had raised her. The woman Mera would call her mother if the name didn't connect to the monster—or bitch—in her head.

"Where should I start?" Ruth asked with a shrug. "Captain Asherath reached our precinct with alarming evidence. We talked to the DA and got a warrant to search Solomon's bank records. We found out he'd taken deposits from the light courts, Summer specially, a day before he went to the authorities with evidence against Fallon. From then on, it was ridiculously easy linking him to several corruption charges."

Mera let out a relieved sigh. "Captain Asherath has been re-instated?"

"With honors. The Commissioner apologized profusely to him. I think he might get a medal." She leaned closer. "He's also been tasked with the mission of cleaning up the Tir Na Nog precinct," she whispered. "Today, Fallon started firing every cop who's dirty. It's been... entertaining."

Mera chuckled. "I'll bet."

"It's also why we've got folks from all boroughs here, at least for the time being," the Cap continued. "Asherath needs help during the transition. He's hired shifters, vamps, witches, and humans to help out, since half of his precinct is basically gone."

"Hmm. The light courts won't take that without a fight."

"That's step number two: cleaning the courts. The Commissioner spoke with the council, and after everything that happened, the fae have officially lost most of their privileges in Tagrad. If they break the law, they'll face the consequences, like the rest of us." The Cap tapped her own temple in a knowing manner. "It's the only way to give Fallon the power to clean up the borough. We can't have detectives bending the law to solve cases. It's madness."

Very true, but things weren't as black and white as they seemed. "Going against the courts might start a civil war."

"We're ready," the Cap assured fearlessly. "The courts talk big, and they might be a threat if they had the support of all their people, but that's not the case. You'd be surprised by the number of lower faeries and Sidhe who already came to us, eager to spill the beans."

"Seriously?"

"Just yesterday, a sprite revealed that the Spring King has been running illegal fighting matches between shifters and vampires. Fallon is gathering evidence to shove him in a cell for the rest of his days. Shouldn't be long now." She grinned wickedly. "Things are looking good, cookie."

Bile swirled in Mera's gut. "What about Summer?"

"We got Zachary's confession on tape, thanks to you and Bast. It only strengthened our case with the Commissioner. I don't think we could've done all of this without the two of you." She smiled proudly at Mera, and tapped her shoulder. "The Summer Court has fallen in shame, which scared Autumn and Spring into compliance. You and Bast basically killed two birds with one stone."

"I see... and where's Bast?" Mera asked, ignoring the dread prickling her chest.

"Finishing up his testimony." A certain sadness befell the Cap's face. "He did kill over twenty Sidhe, cookie. But it was in self-defense, so he'll be cleared soon." She narrowed her eyes at her. "Unless you have something to add?"

Mera tried to hide the sheer panic that came over her.

The image of a black-eyed fae with sharp fangs burst back in her mind. The fae who didn't think twice before killing so many; the fae Mera feared and…

His voice echoed in her memory. *"You didn't run away. I had no choice."*

Bast had murdered those faeries to protect her, and Mera couldn't, even though she should, doom him for that.

"They didn't stop coming at him," she assured, the words bitter on her tongue. "Especially Zachary."

The Cap didn't believe her, Mera recognized that sharp narrowed gaze too well. Ruth studied the top of her head, then her temples. "I wonder how you lost consciousness. You don't have any bruises."

"It was a surge of magic," she blurted. "It knocked me straight out."

The Cap raised a snowy eyebrow. "You? Really?"

Damn it, there might be something wrong with Mera's brain. She'd forgotten that Ruth knew the truth about her. Well, she couldn't go back on her story now. "Zachary's magic was no joke."

The Cap observed her a while longer. "Your new partner said the same."

"How's Jules?" she blurted, hoping to distract her.

Mera's attempt didn't seem to convince her, but the Cap went with it anyway. "Julian stayed behind to cover for me, while I'm helping Fallon sort this mess. It will be a couple of days until I can return, but you should talk to him." She eyed Mera knowingly. "You'll have to tell him at some point, right?"

Yeah, she really would. She and Bast had caught the killer and solved the case, which meant Bast would become her partner.

Permanently.

A cold, bitter sensation knotted in her throat.

Her new partner had savagery and bloodthirst inside him, but so did Mera. For a moment, she worried about what might happen if his darkness came in tune with hers.

"Now that Bast and I are partners…" Mera began, "where will we be located?"

"We're thinking about it." Ruth's gray eyes sparkled. "Fallon and I are discussing how to market your achievement. What you did is a prime example of inter-precinct cooperation, and the Commissioner wants to increase that throughout Hollowcliff. He's calling it the *'Exchange Program: stronger together'*. It's pretty catchy. So, you can expect an interview or two."

'Fantastic,' her siren grumbled.

"It's nothing that could out you as a mermaid, naturally," the Cap guaranteed, although she didn't have to, Mera knew Ruth would never jeopardize her safety.

"About the partner thing…" she asked carefully. "I'm not sure I want to be assigned to Bast."

Crossing her arms, Ruth frowned. "Why? You did stellar work together."

"N-no reason in particular." Mera swallowed. "I just prefer working with Jules."

The Cap leaned forward, studying her. "Sebastian is a handsome male, but I trusted you to keep the siren in check." She blew a sigh filled with disappointment. "If you've slept with him, you must handle the consequences. Nothing I can do about that, especially now."

How dare she!

Well, they did have sex, but in a dream, and that wasn't even the biggest of their problems. The entire situation was a gigantic mess. If Mera told the Cap the truth…

No. She couldn't do that to Bast.

Mera hated him for what he'd done, but she didn't hate him enough to see him in jail, or worse. Besides, telling on him would only raise questions about his motivation, which would lead others back to her, and this time, Ruth wouldn't be able to protect her.

"Okay," Mera agreed. "I'll deal with it."

The Cap cupped her cheek lovingly. "That's the cookie I raised."

A knock came from the door then, and Captain Asherath entered the room. He had dark circles under his eyes, but he didn't seem tired. With his easy smile and relaxed shoulders, he looked more energized than ever.

"Ah, Detective Maurea!" he greeted. "I'm glad you're up. You took a long time to recover from that magic blast."

"How long precisely?"

"A day, give or take."

There was a certain knowledge behind his eyes, something he wasn't saying.

Did he know?

Impossible. Bast had wiped out a small army of fae to protect her secret. She doubted he'd tell Asherath, even if he trusted the fae blindly. Which didn't mean he hadn't told him *something*.

Mera suddenly remembered one face; a bitchy, scrawny complexion. "Before I lost consciousness, Lisandra was alive. Did Bast…"

"Was he forced to kill her?" Captain Asherath rephrased. "No. But she's in pretty bad shape. Losing her husband, her son, and seeing her court crumble… it took a toll on her."

"She lost her mind, cookie," the Cap explained. "We had to send her to an insane asylum. She kept blabbing about the end of days, and how darkness was coming for her."

Mera and Asherath exchanged a knowing glance. Bast played tricks with the mind, Mera had seen it when he'd scrambled with Sara's roommate's memories, so he must've done something to Lisandra.

Mera missed and feared that bastard at the same time, which was insane, but she couldn't deal with that right now. At least Lisandra wasn't dead.

Was her current fate any better, though?

Captain Asherath clapped his hands. "Are you ready to get back on the saddle, as you humans say, Detective Maurea?" He stepped aside and showed her the door. "I could use the help of Hollowcliff's top detectives."

Mera gingerly stood, and the Cap made a move to help her, but stopped midway. This was how Ruth had raised her; always observant yet giving Mera space to do her own thing; to follow her own path.

"I'm ready," she assured, knowing it might be a lie.

She stepped out into the Tir Na Nog precinct, which was packed with police force from every borough.

When they saw her, they started clapping.

It was awkward. The last thing she and Bast deserved was applause.

"May I steal my partner for a moment?" Bast's voice rang from behind, and Mera stilled.

Hell, her entire body froze, but she forced herself to turn around.

Bast stood beside Captain Asherath, and he seemed... different, somehow. Still impossibly handsome, but his piercing blue eyes lacked their usual playfulness.

He avoided staring directly at Mera, and she hated how much that hurt.

"Of course," Captain Asherath said, putting a gentle hand on the Cap's shoulder. "Ruth, we have much to discuss about ongoing cases."

"We sure do." The Cap kissed Mera's forehead. "See you later, cookie."

They left her there, inside a packed precinct with her

partner slash mass-murderer. Mera had never felt lonelier or more vulnerable than right then.

"I guess everything worked out," she told him as she studied her own feet.

"Indeed." Bast took Mera's arm gently, and led her to an empty corridor near the elevator. A muscle jumped in his jaw, his profile harder than stone.

"Kitten, I couldn't let them live," he whispered once they were alone. "It was either you or them, and I made my choice."

Kitten...

Perhaps not all was lost between them.

Perhaps, everything was.

"They couldn't fight back." Her tone sounded helpless and weak. Mera gritted her teeth. "I never took you for a coward, Bast."

He shrugged, either ignoring the insult or faking nonchalance. "If you were so appalled, you should've released them from the macabre sooner."

"I know!" Glancing around, she made sure she hadn't drawn any attention. "I have no clue why it took me so long to release them," she whispered. "I guess a part of me wanted to protect you. Then I realized you didn't need protection at all." She slapped his arm, angry for caring about that monumental dickwart.

He frowned at her, as if she were a puzzle he couldn't decipher. "Mera, I was right, and you know it." He silenced himself, when some vampires walked past them. Bast flicked his hand and the sounds around them waned. "This should give us some privacy."

"You're not a cop," she snapped. "Not on my book. Cops don't mass-murder people without remorse."

He winced as if the words had been blades slashing at him. "Not without remorse. *Never* without remorse."

Mera swallowed dry. As much as she hated admitting it, she shared the responsibility with Bast for the massacre. If she had run away, as he'd asked her to, he wouldn't have needed to kill all the witnesses—and messed with Lisandra's head.

Grunting in annoyance, he crossed his arms. "If you want an apology, you won't get one. I did what I had to do."

"Why?" she blurted. "Why go to such lengths to protect me?" She stepped forward, facing him the way of a bull about to charge. "You wouldn't have killed so many faeries just for anyone."

"Not for anyone, no." He shrugged. "But I guess having a powerful *akritana* in the palm of my hand could be beneficial. Everyone fears your people for a reason." He clicked his tongue. "What you can do…"

Mera stepped back, words failing her. That's why he'd saved her life. Not because he cared⎯maybe he never did.

Bast wanted to use her.

For what?

"Oh, you sneaky bastard." She poked his chest, anger scorching her from the inside. "If you think—"

"I don't think. I *know*. Hate it all you want, kitten, but we're in this together. You crash, I crash." His hooded eyes watched her, and a soft grin hooked on the left side of his cheek. He flicked a string of her hair between his fingers and leaned closer.

Mera should've stepped back, but damn it, she still loved the proximity. Even if she should've known better.

"There's also that thing you told me," he whispered with a low, sensual tone that made desire pool inside her.

She hated him. She hated him so much.

"What thing?"

"You'll remember it eventually, I suppose," he said, his gaze luring her in, obliterating her will to step away. "In the meantime, we should investigate Poseidon and his connection to Sara Hyland."

Mera blinked, finally free of his pull.

"Yes." She cleared her throat and stepped back. "Someone from Atlantea got Sara Hyland pregnant. Zachary was there to kill her, probably with magic, but they glamoured him into drowning her instead."

Bast nodded. "How is that any different from killing her another way?"

"It isn't. I think they wanted to watch it and make sure she was dead. Zachary mentioned seeing a drone, but he'd dismissed it as losing his mind." She shook her head. "How could a drone have glamoured him? It has no magic. And to top it up, Poseidon isn't real."

"Which means we might have a maniac who thinks he's a god on our hands." Bast blew air through his lips. "Great."

Mera didn't want to work another case with this deceiving asshole, but she didn't have a choice.

You crash, I crash... Partner.

"We must be careful on this one," he urged. "We have to make sure none of it links back to you."

"Why would it?" She slammed her hands on her waist. "I don't know any maniacs with gigantic egos. Oh, wait." She gave him a ferocious grin.

Bast rolled his eyes and was ready for a comeback when someone spoke from behind him.

"Sebastian?"

Bast's spine snapped straight, shock taking over his face. Slowly, he turned around to face a faerie clad in a long dress of the finest black silk. Glittering diamonds attached to the fabric made it resemble the night sky.

The fae wore a long dark veil on her head, which she pulled back to show her face.

Her pale skin contrasted with her black attire, and her

hair was the color of the moon, like Bast's. They also shared the same high cheekbones and straight nose, but their eyes were different. Hers was a deep pink that made her seem more otherworldly than usual for a faerie.

"*Amma?*" he muttered, like he couldn't believe she was there. As if making sure she wasn't a dream.

Amma. It meant mom, which differed from mother. *Amma* was informal and implied love. *Imma*, Mother, implied... detachment. Fear and respect.

That particular lesson in Faeish, Mera would never forget.

"Sebastian," she croaked, holding back tears. "Your father is dead."

"I heard. What are you doing here?"

Bast took her in his arms, the woman small and frail against his tall, strong frame. He rested a hand over the top of her head, the gentleness making the killer, *death bringer*, seem vulnerable and kind.

But he wouldn't fool Mera. Not anymore.

"You didn't come to the funeral." The fae let out a muffled sob against his chest.

"I had my reasons, *amma*," he quietly confessed.

His mother let herself cry for a moment, then took a deep breath, slowly recomposing. She wiped tears from her cheeks, her pink eyes glistening. "I understand. The bird flies his own path..." She stared at no point in particular.

"Amma?" Bast asked, and his mother seemed to blink back into herself. "What's wrong?"

"I... I need your help." She sniffed, her eyes a bit hollow. Like only half of her was really there. "Someone murdered him."

"Father died of natural causes," Bast spoke softly, the way one would when speaking to a child. "That's what the report said, remember?"

When did he find time to read a report about his father's death? Perhaps Bast cared more about him than he let others see.

Not that Mera gave a shit.

She hated her partner, even if sympathy for his loss pushed its way through that red, burning layer she'd wrapped around her heart.

"No, Sebastian. The Night King was murdered," his mother whispered, glancing around to make sure no one had listened. "And you must bring his killer to justice."

Find out what happens next in *TO KILL A KING*, book 2 of the Hollowcliff Detectives series.

If you enjoyed this book, do consider leaving a review. They make an author's day!

You can also join the Wildlings to get a FREE copy of BLESSED LIGHT, an urban fantasy romance novel.

AN EXCLUSIVE GIFT

Join C.S. Wilde's mailing list to receive an exclusive monthly serial. Just go to **www.subscribepage.com/liam**

Be sure to check out C.S. Wilde's bestselling Urban Fantasy Romance series,
BLESSED FURY
Out now!

Be sure to check out C.S. Wilde's Sci-fi Romance series,
FROM THE STARS
Out now!

ACKNOWLEDGMENTS

A huge thanks to my book cover designer, Juan at Covers by Juan, and my brilliant editors Christina Walker at Supernatural Editing, and Stephany Wallace.

Another huge thanks to my husband, which comes as no surprise to him since I thank him in all my books. Without him, none of these stories would see the light of day.

Shout out to my beta readers and ARC reviewers who have shown this book so much love. You all kick major ass.

Lastly, thank you, reader, who at this point is getting extra points for making it all the way here. I hope you enjoyed reading this story. Also, if it weren't for you, this book would be just words scrambled on a bunch of pages, so thank you for letting me bring these characters to life in your head. Which is creepy and slightly invasive if you think about it, but still pretty awesome.

THANKS FOR READING!

Choose which book you want next!

Ratings help me determine which series I'll prioritize, so if you can't wait for the next book in this series, leave a review and show your love. I never leave series unfinished, but your input will determine how quickly I'll start working on the next book.

That's right: YOU get to choose which books come next by leaving a review.

Yay!

Another aspect that helps me decide which books come next is sales. So if you acquired this book through piracy, make sure to buy your copy.

Piracy is not only a crime punishable by fines and federal imprisonment, but it also ensures that no more books in this series will be written.

Piracy ruins books. It ruins authors too. And that's not cool at all.

Keep up to date with the latest news and release dates by joining C.S. Wilde's mailing list

And if you want to discuss all things Mera and Bast, join the Wildlings or follow C.S. Wilde on Facebook!

ALSO BY C.S. WILDE

Hollowcliff Detectives:
TO KILL A FAE
TO KILL A KING
TO KILL THE DEAD
TO KILL A GOD

Angels of Fate Series:
BLESSED LIGHT *(Angels of Fate Prequel)*
BLESSED FURY *(Angels of Fate book 1)*
CURSED DARKNESS *(Angels of Fate book 2)*
BOOK 3 *(Coming in 2020)*

Science Fiction Romance:
FROM THE STARS *(The Dimensions series book 1)*
BEYOND THE STARS *(The Dimensions series book 2)*
ACROSS THE STARS *(The Dimensions series book 3)*
The Dimensions Series Boxset *(Get book 1 for free with the boxset)*

Urban Fantasy Romance:
SWORD WITCH

Paranormal Thriller Adventure:
A COURTROOM OF ASHES

ABOUT THE AUTHOR

C. S. Wilde wrote her first Fantasy novel when she was eight. That book was absolutely terrible, but her mother told her it was awesome, so she kept writing.

Now a grown up (though many will beg to differ), C. S. Wilde writes about fantastic worlds, love stories larger than life and epic battles.

She also, quite obviously, sucks at writing an author bio. She finds it awkward that she must write this in the third person and hopes you won't notice.

For up to date promotions and release dates of upcoming books, sign up for the latest news at www.cswilde.com. You can also connect on twitter via @thatcswilde or on facebook at C.S. Wilde.

You can also join the Wildlings, C.S. Wilde's exclusive Facebook group.

Printed in Poland
by Amazon Fulfillment
Poland Sp. z o.o., Wrocław

25305181R10147